All the Little Things

Heidi Dischler

Other books by Heidi Dischler:

Words We Never Say

2,697 Pages

ALL THE LITTLE THINGS
Copyright © 2022 by Heidi Dischler

Printed in the United States of America

First Printing, October 1, 2022

ISBN: 9798843036126

Book Cover Design by Heidi Dischler

Check out the author's website!
www.HeidiDischler.com

"Things turn out best for the people who make the best of the way things turn out."

—John Wooden

This one's for me.

Chapter 1

She wasn't exactly sure how it had all started that morning. Caroline had smiled at Izzy, walked down the hallway of their school where everything was okay. She was okay. Until the hallway emptied. Until she was left alone.

Breathe.

You're alone.

You're going to die.

She had ended up in the backseat of her car as she so often had. She couldn't smile anymore. Couldn't hide it anymore.

So, she had held her knees and rocked herself as the darkness set in.

Just be normal, Caroline.

Fix it.

She could fix it when other people were around. She could always be okay when she wasn't alone.

Alonealonealone.

You're going to die.

Fix it.

Her chest had gotten tight. It had been so hard to breathe. Black spots had floated across her vision.

She had been choking. She had thought she was dying. She could still feel the dried tears on her cheeks if she just reached up to touch—

"Caroline?" Dr. B said, her voice sounding far away.

Caroline wanted to say it all out loud. All of the ways that she was falling apart inside. She was so deep in her thoughts—the monotony of the day—thinking about being alone and dying and all the different ways that people leave you. She knew she wasn't in the backseat of her car anymore. She knew she wasn't alone or in any danger. She kept telling herself she wasn't going to die. Although, she couldn't stop thinking about the 150,000 people who died that day. From accidents, diseases, allergic reactions, overdoses, and other fatal health issues. Medicine that was supposed to help them had death listed as a side effect. Medicine that was supposed to work, to make them better, could kill them.

150,000 people a day. All dead, and nothing anyone could do to stop it. She had been wanting to tell someone that for the better part of six months, but she couldn't exactly say that to her therapist. With all of those different ways to die, only 150,000 people died each day of the almost eight billion who populated the world. Why, then, had it happened to *her* mother?

Caroline pulled her eyes away from the brightly painted yellow walls and looked over to the woman sitting across from her. "Huh?"

The older woman smiled at Caroline and shook her head. "I asked how school has been."

Caroline could see the kindness in Dr. B's eyes. That was always the first thing she noticed about her.

There was so much kindness, but Caroline never could find a reason to open up about anything that was important. "Oh, you know," Caroline started, "it's been great. Being the editor for the yearbook is amazing. Having half days is literally like the best part, though. Especially on Fridays." She looked over to Dr. B to see her reaction. Caroline didn't mean to be so sarcastic. It just kind of... happened. Especially since she spent her Fridays in that brightly colored prison.

As she waited for Dr. B's reaction, she imagined the yellow wallpaper peeling away, strip by strip. She wondered what color would be underneath. Probably black.

"You seem a little flustered today," Dr. B started.

"Yeah, I just—well, I need to go home for lunch today to check the mail and eat. I guess I'm just antsy." She decided not to mention that she went home every day for lunch and it was usually just to check the mail.

"Caroline?"

"Yes?"

"Your grandparents tell me that you're staying in town to attend the community college here. I thought you wanted to go to your mother's college? FSU?"

Caroline's back stiffened. She should have known that they would tell her about this. "I think the community college will be better for me. They have a great pharmacy tech program that I can do. I can stay close to Grams and Gramps and work at the pharmacy." Caroline tried to say it in a tone that should exude her excitement, but she doubted it came out very well.

"The pharmacy technician program is great, but what about pharmacy school? Your grandparents seem to remember that was all you could talk about before your mother passed."

Caroline flinched. She couldn't help it. She hated when people talked about her mom. "That was half a year ago, Dr. B. Things change." She tried not to have a condescending tone because she knew it would just get her in trouble, but she needed her to stop asking questions about college.

"How long have we been having these sessions, Caroline?"

"Um, a little over six months I guess?"

"Do you feel like they are helping you?"

No. "Yes, of course," Caroline smiled, but she could feel the bile rising up in her stomach.

Dr. B sighed. It was one of those deep, chest-opening sighs that made Caroline feel small and insignificant. "You don't have to tell me what I want to hear, you know?"

Caroline studied the woman. Her silvery hair was tied back in a clean bun on the back of her head. Completely opposite from the messy ones Caroline normally secured on the top of her head. The silver in Dr. B's hair made her seem so much older than she actually looked. If Caroline had to guess only on facial features, she would have to say that Dr. B was probably in her early to mid-forties.

She noticed that Dr. B was waiting on an answer.

"Oh, sorry," Caroline started. "I thought the question was rhetorical." She shimmied in her seat a bit, getting uncomfortable, feeling heat all over her body. "Well, anyway. I have to go now. Can't be late for my shift at the pharmacy." Caroline smiled cheerfully at the woman and waved goodbye, grabbing her things to make a quick exit.

"Hold on, Caroline, we still have a few minutes," Dr. B said, and even though Caroline desperately wanted to leave, she couldn't be that rude. So, she turned around to face the woman.

"Did you get the refill for your prescription? Do you feel like the medicine is helping?"

Caroline felt the tingles creeping up her fingers as she tried to calm herself down. She didn't want to talk about this. She didn't want to be here. "I think it's working," Caroline said, but the flat tone gave her away.

"One last thing," Dr. B said as she stood up to walk over to Caroline. She stared down at Caroline's clenched fists and sighed deeply. Sadness crinkled around her brows. Caroline didn't want her sadness. "Do you remember the breathing exercises we talked about?"

Caroline wanted to cry. It always came on suddenly and without warning, but happened often when she felt overwhelmed.

"In through the nose," Dr. B inhaled.

One. Two. Three. Four.

"Out through the mouth," Dr. B exhaled.

One. Two. Three. Four.

They repeated this again, and even if the tingling sensation creeping up her fingers had gone away, the absolute defeat she felt was stronger than ever. She felt weak. Broken. As if she weren't a whole person.

"I'm fine," Caroline said after the breathing exercise was over, though her shoulders were tense and her muscles taut.

Dr. B nodded, both an acknowledgement and a release.

Caroline hurriedly took one last look at the room before she left. All she could imagine was the black paint underneath all that yellow.

***

Sitting in her car, Caroline took a deep breath. She hated Fridays. Absolutely despised them because it was so much harder to put up a façade for someone who was trained to see behind it. She rested her head on the steering wheel and turned the heater on to full blast. Her right leg began bouncing up and down as she felt the nervous energy buzzing through her veins. It wasn't even that cold outside, but all Caroline wanted was to feel the Arizona heat piercing through her skin, destroying that buzz. Too bad it was the middle of January and the hottest it ever got was still—at the very minimum—cardigan weather.

As the heat hit her in the face with her forehead still against the steering wheel, Caroline pulled out her phone and opened the single most important app on it: Color Sorter. All Caroline had to do was focus on the colors, moving them from one vial to another until all the colorful balls of the same color were in the same vial. She only had to focus on the colors and the heat. Not college. Not her mom. Not breathing exercises. Not anything else but the heat and the colors.

As the heat got unbearable, Caroline felt as if she couldn't breathe. At least there was a reason, though. At least she knew the source and could fix it. She strained to get a full breath of air, taking a deep, quivering inhale. She began to chew on her lip as she sorted more and more colors.

Right when she thought she couldn't take it anymore, she turned the AC on and waited as the cool air filled her car.

There. She could breathe again. She fixed it.

I fixed it.

So, as she took in full breaths of cool air, she drove away from the yellow walls, and the Fridays, and drove towards her grandparents' house. Instead of going inside when she got there, she simply pulled up to the mailbox and took out its contents.

Inside, there were three letters for her, each from a different college around the country. She put her grandparents mail back inside the mailbox, taking her letters with her. She didn't really want to know which colleges they were from. She didn't really want to even know if she got accepted. She just wanted to make sure that her grandparents did *not* see any of them.

Caroline stuffed the letters in her glove compartment, and then drove away, not bothering to pick up lunch.

When she got to the pharmacy, she stared up at the sign with its vintage lettering:

Campbell's Pharmacy

It made her feel safe and secure and everything that she didn't feel when she tried to leave that small town. How had she become so thoroughly trapped? And it wasn't like she was forced to stay there. It wasn't like someone was telling her that she didn't have other options. She had done it to herself—let the darkness in, let it consume her—and now the darkness wouldn't let her leave.

She shook herself out of her thoughts and got ready to go inside her grandparents' pharmacy. Curtis was working today, so at least she wouldn't be alone, which was always a plus in her opinion.

Curtis was in his mid-twenties, an aspiring film critic, and gave totally great advice despite not having much life experience. He had gone to the community college and got his pharmacy technician certificate—which is where Caroline got the idea in the first place—but after working for a few years, he realized his passion was movies.

"Afternoon, Curtis," Caroline said with a smile as she walked behind the counter, slipped on her Campbell's Pharmacy vest, and clocked in.

"Afternoon, Caroline," Curtis said, almost monotonal.

"Have you smiled at anyone today?" she asked, still wearing her cheery Caroline face.

"Nope," he said as he grabbed a few filled prescriptions and filed them by last name.

"Can I be the first person?" she joked.

He basically rolled his neck as he rolled his eyes. "No."

"You can't not smile at me forever, Curtis."

"Watch me."

"You won't succeed," she sang as she went to the back to package prescriptions. Out of the corner of her eye, she could see him grin and it made her smile.

In the back, the prescriptions sat in baskets, labeled with names and dosages and information. She took the first one, looked at the baby blue color of the pills inside the little orange bottle, and got on the computer to look up the prescription. She found the corresponding drug facts sheet and packaged the medicine in a little white bag. As she did this, she read the warnings, side effects, and uses of the drug. It's something that she got in the habit of doing about six months ago and had just never stopped. It was surprising to her how many drugs listed death as a side effect. It had always been ironic to her that something that was supposed to make you better could potentially make you worse.

Once it was packaged, she moved on to the next one and kept going after that. She got to her own prescription, packaged it, and stuffed it in her bag. She listed on the computer that it was picked up, so her grandparents—Grams specifically—would know that she was still refilling her prescription. The bile from earlier that day came back, and Caroline swallowed to get rid of the lump in her throat as she tried to continue packaging other people's prescriptions.

When the bile just wouldn't go away, she stopped working so she could write a list.

<u>How to Hide the Darkness</u>
1. Be nice to people.
2. Smile.
3. Stop thinking.
4. Never let yourself be alone.
5. Don't mention college.

The list helped her to calm down. Writing lists always seemed to do that for her.

Before she knew it, it was five o'clock, so she took her break and went to the counter to see Curtis.

"Catch," she said, tossing candy to Curtis. It was his favorite chocolate bar. She grabbed a bag of chips to eat as well.

His face started twitching as a smile formed on his lips. He shook his head and laughed. "Damn you, Caroline."

"Cheery Caro at your service," she said with flourish and a bow.

"More like cheesy," he said, the scowl back on his face. "Have you gotten all of your college acceptance letters back yet?"

She tried not to frown, but it happened anyway. She jinxed herself by writing that list....

"Uh oh," he started. "What is it?"

"Nothing," she said as she shook her head and smiled. "Didn't Gramps tell you that I'm getting certified as a pharmacy tech at the community college?"

"Caroline," he said, "you could go to med school. You could be a pharmacist like your grandfather. You could probably do anything you wanted."

"This *is* what I want, Curtis. Just like you want to be a film critic," Caroline smiled at him brightly, and started walking away so she didn't have to continue that conversation. She turned her head back quickly to say, "Now eat your candy bar before I take it back!"

In the back room, Caroline closed her eyes and took a deep breath. She was so tired of having those conversations. It was like once someone got to a certain age, all anyone could ever ask them about was college.

So, she opened the bag of chips and began eating, hoping that sour feeling in her stomach would go away. Caroline hadn't been in the back room for more than thirty minutes when she heard her name being called.

"Caroline! Caroline—hi, Curtis—Caro*line*!"

She shook her head and chuckled, her nerves beginning to ease. Izzy busted through the doors, arms gesturing wildly into the air. "What are you doing working?"

"Iz, it's Friday. I always work on Fridays," Caroline laughed.

"Valentine's Day is *Monday*. I have nothing picked out to wear and you're working? Nick is going to send me flowers during second hour, so I need to look perfect." Izzy exuded the vibrance and bubbly nature that Caroline loved, keeping her sane and happy. Being around her kept Caroline smiling more than anyone else, too.

"I get off in about half an hour. We can go dig through my closet after that," she said with a smile as she handed Izzy a basket full of prescriptions to bring to the front desk.

"Oh, thank you, Caro. You are a saint."

Iz walked with her to the front desk, set the basket down, and began talking to Curtis. "The film critic scowl looks horrible on you, Curtis," Izzy said as she leaned on the counter, studying the candy.

Caroline grabbed the gummy worms and handed them to Izzy, marking it down on her tab along with Curtis' candy bar and her chips from earlier. Izzy lit up, stood up straight, and began eating the worms.

"You think so?" Curtis asked as he stretched his face muscles. "I'm trying to practice the face I'll make when I see a movie I don't like."

"Good luck with that," Caroline chimed in.

So far, there hadn't been a movie that Curtis had watched that he hadn't liked. Iz and Caroline had tried telling him, but it was hard to be a film critic if you couldn't critique a single movie you watched. Even the movies that were supposed to be bad Curtis found to be "cinematic masterpieces."

"There will be one someday," Curtis said, readjusting the frown on his face. "And when I find it, I'll know that I'm ready."

Caroline and Izzy glanced at each other and tried not to laugh. He glared at them as he walked around the side of the front desk to hang up his pharmacy vest. He clocked out and saluted them as he left.

"Goodbye Isabelle, the gummy worm eater, and Caroline, the pharmacy technician," Curtis said as he walked out the door.

"Ha," Caroline said. She tried to laugh but couldn't make herself do it.

"Caro," Iz said with a smile, redirecting her attention. "Let's talk about my outfit."

Caroline shook her head and completely pushed away the thoughts that Curtis' comment had brought forward. It was always easy with Izzy.

Caroline was happy—she knew that she was—but as soon as she was alone, something always changed. The darkness always crept up on her and wouldn't let her go.

Chapter 2

As Caroline pulled up to her grandparents' house, she stuffed the three letters from earlier into her backpack right next to her prescription. Once she got out of her car, Izzy walked inside with her to the smell of pork roast hitting them both. Caroline heard Izzy's stomach growl and laughed, but as soon as she did, her stomach growled as well. Izzy gave her a look and Caroline shrugged.

"Hey, Grams!" Caroline said as she and Iz walked into the kitchen.

"Hi, sweetie," Grams said as Caroline kissed her cheek. "Hello, Isabelle. How was school today?"

"Exhausting," Izzy sighed as she slumped into a wooden chair at the dining table.

"It was okay," Caroline smiled, rolling her eyes at Iz. "She's overexaggerating. We hardly do anything at school right now."

"That's because you girls are seniors," Grams said with pride.

"It smells so good in here, Grams." Izzy stood to look at the roast Grams was cutting.

"That's because Grams, here, is an amazing cook," Gramps said as he walked through the front door. He walked over to Grams and gave her a kiss on the top of her head.

"Literally, my favorite couple ever," Izzy sighed.

"What were you up to today, Gramps?" Caroline asked as she gave him a hug. "I didn't see you at the pharmacy."

He smiled as he sat down next to Izzy, gave her shoulder a pat, and said, "Just a check-up at the doctor's office." Caroline's heart skipped a beat before he added, "Nothing to worry about. Your grams keeps me as healthy as a horse." Gramps rubbed his tight button down shirt with his swollen belly and brightened as a plate of pork roast with carrots and potatoes was placed in front of him.

Grams placed a plate in front of Iz and Caroline, then sat down at her own place at the table. "You could probably afford to be a little less healthy, dear," Grams said with a smile. Gramps laughed as he took a bite of his food.

Caroline took her first bite slowly. Her nerves from the day and her therapy session almost always killed her appetite. She knew, though, if she didn't eat they'd ask questions. They'd talk to Dr. B about it. So, she took another bite. She turned to Izzy, who had already eaten half of her plate before Caroline even ate four bites. "Iz, jeez, slow down," Caroline laughed, the darkness going away.

"Look, Caro," she began as she ate another potato slice, "my parents *never* cook like this at home. I need this more than you do."

"I think the ironic part about that statement is that your parents *do* cook like this at home," Caroline said under her breath.

Izzy glared at her and everyone laughed as Iz got up to make a second plate of food. Grams beamed, though, because she loved when Izzy came over. Izzy always ate at least two plates and was more enthusiastic about Grams' cooking than anyone Caroline had ever known.

***

After supper, Izzy and Caroline had done the dishes and headed upstairs to check out Caroline's closet. Izzy pulled out various pieces of clothing in pinks, reds, and whites, dumping them all onto the bed where Caroline was currently sitting. She had to wonder—with Izzy's extensive wardrobe and all— how she ever even needed to borrow clothes from her.

"I am still sitting here," Caroline said as a light pink tank top landed on her head.

Izzy turned around and grinned. "Oh, sorry, Caro," she said as she took the top off her head and placed it on the pile of clothes beside her. "I'm just nervous, you know?" Izzy sighed and Caroline felt as if she were looking at herself. Izzy hardly ever got nervous, so Caroline easily understood just how important this was to her. She sat next to Caroline and laid her head on Caroline's shoulder. Caroline began to play with Izzy's long, black ponytail.

"Nick and I have been together for a year now. I just want to look perfect and… I mean, Caro, I think I'm falling in love with him."

Caroline stopped playing with her hair and picked Izzy's head up to face her. "Whoa," Caroline started. "I mean, Iz, what about college? Don't you want to go to South Carolina?"

She stayed quiet for a moment. "I mean, yeah, but that's months away. We still have time to figure it out."

"Don't you have to start registering for classes in May? That's only three months away...."

"Ugh, I know," Izzy groaned. She stood abruptly and shook her head. "It doesn't matter, I'll figure it out." She began rummaging through the pile of clothes and pulled out a silky red top. "Ah ha! This is the one. I have a black leather skirt and I'll wear it with a cute jean jacket or something. What do you think?" She held it up against her body and twirled.

Caroline sighed and smiled despite herself. "Gorgeous, of course."

***

After Izzy had left around eight, Caroline laid down in bed and started staring at the ceiling. It had been hours—she was sure of it—but she couldn't seem to get her brain to turn off. She couldn't stop thinking about college and her prescription and the pharmacy tech program and doing better than just being a tech and pharmacy school and FSU....

She turned over to lay on her right side, hoping that would quiet her mind. Of course it didn't, though.

What if she didn't *want* to do better? What if she just wanted to stay in Arizona with her grandparents, with the safety and the feeling of calm that she got when she got home? Seeing Izzy and Grams and Gramps and Curtis and just staying at home, it all made her safe from the darkness. But none of them would ever let her forget that she could do better— that she could go further. It all just made her want to puke and kept her mind on that stupid drawer in her desk.

Caroline groaned and rolled over to grab her phone. She kicked the covers off her and started playing the color sorting app.

Mom would've wanted you to go to pharmacy school.

She would've wanted more for you.

Caroline closed the app and turned on her music as loud as the phone would let her. Then she opened the app again and kept playing.

Mom knew that she wanted to go to FSU.

Mom would've made Caroline go because it's what she wanted most ever since she was a little girl.

Mom wasn't there, though.

Caroline stood up abruptly and squeezed her eyes shut, pressing the palms of her hands into her eyes. "Stop it, Caroline," she said to herself. "You're okay. Everything is okay."

She felt the darkness creeping up and she wanted to stop it. She wanted to make it go away—to fix it— but she couldn't fix this. Not like she could fix the air in her car, simply turning a dial to make it easier to breathe.

She went over to her backpack and took out her prescription and the mail that she had gotten today at lunch. Caroline opened the prescription package, took the bottle, and went to her bathroom. She put the bottle in her medicine cabinet next to the six other bottles. The next thing she had to do was a little harder. She had to look at the letters. She knew that if she didn't look at them, she would never sleep. She had to see them even if it made everything hurt that much more.

Caroline brought the three letters to her desk and sat down. She opened the first one.

Dear Caroline Roland,
Congratulations! You have been accepted into....

She quickly opened the bottom right drawer in her desk and threw the letter in. Caroline felt her chest tightening. She felt the muscles around her lungs aching as they tried to expand, to take in the air that she so desperately needed but never seemed to get enough of. She rested her elbows on the desk and held her forehead with both hands. A small squeak escaped from Caroline's lips and she quickly put her hands over her mouth. She slowly shook as she took a deep breath in and continued opening the letters.

Dear Caroline Roland,
Congratulations! You have been accepted into....

Caroline threw this one into the drawer, too, as she began opening the last one. Her fingers shook as she slowly ripped the envelope.

Dear Caroline Roland,
Congratulations! It is with great pleasure that we
wish to extend an offer to attend....

She wanted to scream. Why was she doing this to herself? Why apply to all of these schools she knew that she'd never go to? Why dream about them when she knew that she could never leave? Getting accepted into college wasn't the problem. It never had been. Ever since six months ago, school seemed to be the only thing she could focus on. Her grades were good. Really good. The real problem was much deeper, more visceral and raw and irreparable. So, instead of thinking about those problems, Caroline began writing a list:

All the Reasons Why Going to Arizona State Community College is a Good Idea
1. I would be able to stay close to home.
2. I'd be able to work at the pharmacy fulltime.
3. I could take care of Grams and Gramps.
4. I would save money.
5. I would never have to feel the darkness once the college decision was made.
6. Everyone knows everyone in Valor City, Arizona.
7. I'd never have to think about dying alone again.

She ripped the list off of her writing pad, put it on top of all the acceptance letters, shut the drawer, and grabbed her phone and a blanket. She just needed to clear her head.

As she walked out the back door, she felt the chill settle into her bones. It felt good to feel something that wasn't just inside her head.

Caroline walked up to the gate in the backyard. As she opened it, she imagined leaving Arizona, leaving everything that was wrong with her behind. She thought about going to FSU— thought about her mom and her dad, how they met there—and she knew it was too late to stop the darkness and to stop herself.

She closed the gate behind her and walked over to the patch of grass that was indented with her shape. Caroline wrapped the blanket around herself and sat down. This was the furthest she'd ever get. It was the only place she could go that made her feel as if she was actually *going* somewhere. It was there that she sat on the state line. It was there that she crossed over into Utah and could be in a different place that wasn't a pharmacy tech program, that wasn't a life that she didn't want.

Caroline began to feel her jaw quiver. She started to open her phone to play the color sorting app, but set it down beside her instead. She wrapped her arms around her knees and rested her head on them, letting out the tears that always seemed to be hiding just behind her eyes.

"I miss you, Mom," she squeaked as the tears took over her voice.

Tomorrow was a new day, she had to remind herself of that. It would get better. *It had to get better.* There was a track meet tomorrow morning that she had to take pictures for. She could hang out with Iz and make the darkness disappear. She could spend time with her grandparents. She could make it.

She could.

Chapter 3

She couldn't. She definitely couldn't get out of bed the next morning. The sunlight was coming in through the curtains and it was blinding her. She groaned and rolled over, pulling the covers further over her head.

"Caroline!" Grams called up the stairs. "Breakfast is ready."

She squeezed her eyes shut so tightly that she began to see colors behind her eyelids. It was a Saturday. She shouldn't have to get out of bed for breakfast. She shouldn't have to do anything. Except, of course, take pictures for the yearbook. There was the track meet and she couldn't miss it. Not to mention she never could find it in her heart to tell her Grams or Gramps no for anything.

So, Caroline threw on some baggy sweatpants that were tight at her ankles, a fitted long sleeve shirt, her white sneakers, and a big over-sized cardigan. If she was gonna go anywhere today, she might as well be as comfortable as she could be. She quickly put her hair up into a messy bun and tried to put on a little mascara and concealer so she didn't look like a complete zombie. It was no use, though. With less than two hours of sleep, being a part of the walking dead was inevitable.

When she finally went downstairs, it was already eight o'clock and the meet would start at nine. She didn't have much time to eat, so she grabbed a few pieces of toast and began to head out.

"You're not going to eat more than that?" Grams asked. Her hands were on her hips and Caroline could tell that she wasn't happy with her recent breakfast decision.

"I'm late?" Caroline said it as a question, half-smiling and shrugging her shoulders. She quickly grabbed a piece of bacon and put it in her mouth to appease her grandmother.

Grams shook her head at Caroline and shooed her away with a wave of her hand. Caroline didn't wait another second, not trusting her Grams not to change her mind about the breakfast situation.

As Caroline sat in her car, driving to the track meet with two pieces of toast on her lap, she munched slowly, trying to make it last as long as she possibly could.

When the toast was gone and she had parked in the school parking lot, she quickly texted Izzy to find out where she was. Caroline went to the trunk of her car and took her camera out of her camera case. She adjusted the lens and took a few pictures to find the best settings for that lighting. Once she felt it was as good as it would get, she finally walked over to the track and found Izzy stretching near the back of the team.

"Caro!" Izzy called when she saw Caroline approaching. She ran up to hug her even though it had only been a few hours since the two had interacted.

Izzy was dressed in her track uniform, her black hair pulled into a sleek ponytail on top of her head. She was smiling brightly, ready to sprint. Izzy did the 100 meter sprint and she was the best the track team had seen in a long time. Caroline used to do the 1500 meter. She found it ironic how well their different distances perfectly portrayed their differences in personalities.

"You know," Izzy started, and Caroline could already feel the pit forming in her stomach. "You should be here with us."

Caroline laughed it off, trying to feign nonchalance. "I *am* here."

"You know what I mean, Caroline," Izzy said, getting serious.

"I just—" Caroline started. "I couldn't run this year." What a funny statement to say out loud especially since all Caroline had been doing those past six months was running. "But c'mon," Caroline said, "pose for the yearbook."

Izzy couldn't help but to smile as she shook her head. She did her best "athlete" pose and Caroline raised the camera to her face to take a picture.

"Now go over there and help us win the meet," Caroline said as she ushered Izzy away.

When Izzy was finally gone, Caroline stepped off the track so that they could get ready for the first heat. She put the strap of the camera around her neck and brought it back up to her face, aiming it towards the runners. She snapped a few pictures, watched as they ran, listened to the *thump thump thump* of their feet on the track. She let the camera fall loosely down to her abdomen. She closed her eyes tightly and breathed in through her nose. Out through her mouth.

One. Two. Three. Four.

When she finally opened her eyes, she put the camera back up to her face, feeling its cold plastic resting on her cheek. Caroline aimed towards the audience and saw someone she recognized walking towards her. She snapped a few pictures, and then moved the camera away from her face, blinking a few times to get her eyes to focus.

He was smiling at her as he walked towards her. "Bennett?" she said. "Oh my gosh," she continued, a smile spreading across her face. "Bennett freaking Williams." She jogged up to him the rest of the way and tried to give him a hug. The camera got smushed in between them and he quickly stepped back.

"Oh, sorry," he said with a nervous laugh.

Caroline tried to move the camera to hug him, but that didn't work either. So, she just ended up giving him a side hug. Then it was just awkward.

Bennett rubbed the back of his neck, his black-rimmed glasses falling down his nose. He pushed them back up, and then looked at her. "So, how have you been?"

"Good," she smiled, hearing the cheeriness in her own voice and wondering where the heck it came from. "I thought you were in Massachusetts for college?"

"I came back in the fall for an internship close to home. I've been overloaded with work and the internship just ended, so I finally got the chance to hang out with real people."

"So lawyers don't count?" Caroline joked.

Bennett blushed and shook his head. "That's not what I meant," he chuckled nervously.

"You know I'm just teasing," she said as she lightly punched him. "Jeez, it's just been so long. When was the last time I saw you? I think it was like my sophomore year?"

He nodded, "Yeah, it was."

They got quiet as they both just stared at each other for a moment. Caroline couldn't get the smile off her face, which felt so weird compared to how she'd been lately. Bennett looked so nerdy and goofy and adorable just in the same way Caroline remembered him. Except older. And maybe better looking?

"So, why aren't you on the track?" Bennett asked.

It definitely was the wrong question. After hearing it from Izzy, and then getting asked by Bennett, Caroline felt her smile deflate a bit. "Oh," she started quietly. "I just...." She tried to think of a good excuse—a way to bounce back. It came to her all in a flash. "I've been focusing more on yearbook this year. I'm the editor, you know," she said cockily.

He raised his eyebrows and laughed. "Oh really now?"

"Yep. I get to boss everyone around. It's pretty great."

"I bet it is. You never were very far from that camera."

They got quiet again. Caroline tried to think of something to ask him, but her head was swimming. She wanted to keep the conversation going, but her thoughts were fuzzy and she just kept... staring.

Bennett rubbed the back of his neck again, smiling nervously. "Would you—I mean, do you think...?" He laughed and took a deep breath. "Would you maybe want to go get coffee after this?"

The smile that grew on Caroline's face was outrageous. "I would love that, Bennett," she said, trying to contain her giddiness. "But, on one condition."

Bennett's shoulders tensed as his eyebrows crinkled in confusion.

"Say cheese!" Caroline laughed as she brought the camera to her face and took the single most greatest picture of an unsuspecting Bennett Williams.

***

When Caroline and Bennett left together, one of the hardest things—to Caroline, at least—was getting past Izzy. The amount of eyebrow-raises and half-smirks and the "Oh, so you're going to get coffee, right?" that she had asked at least three times were downright embarrassing. Caroline loved her for it, though, and she thought it made Bennett more embarrassed than her. She secretly loved that, too.

So, there they were, sitting across from each other in the café, both sipping on coffee at lunchtime. When they had went to get their orders taken, Bennett had bought her coffee and a cookies 'n cream parfait that she had been eyeing, and he paid without a second thought. Caroline didn't even have time to protest before he was done.

"Are you sure you don't want a bite?" Caroline asked again as she put another spoonful of the whipped masterpiece in her mouth.

Bennett laughed at her and shook his head. "You really haven't changed at all."

Caroline laughed a secret, darker laugh to herself as she stared down at her parfait. When she looked back up, he was eyeing her curiously.

Bennett shifted in his seat a little. "I shouldn't have said that. You just—" He rubbed the back of his neck and smiled sadly. "I'm sorry about your mom."

Caroline nodded, feeling almost relieved that he had noticed her. That he had noticed something other than what she wanted him to. "I'm sorry about your brother."

It was Bennett's turn then to sadly smile down at his coffee. "I guess we have that in common then. Not really different from the last time, but not really the same either."

She smiled then, thinking back to all the different ways she had tried to get him to notice her sophomore year of high school (and his senior year). He had always been so adorably nerdy in the most endearing way. He was also—even then—the kindest high school boy she had ever met. "You always did sound so poetic, Bennett Ryan Williams." Caroline blushed furiously then, realizing that she had used his middle name.

"You remember my middle name?" he laughed.

She tried to feign nonchalance but it didn't work. So she just bit her lip as she tried to hide the smile that easily took over her features. "It was the art class we took together. Remember? Mrs. Ramirez asked us to spell out our full name on a piece of paper. We passed them around and everyone had to put three things that they liked about that person using the first letters of that person's name."

Bennett's smile grew just as much as Caroline's did. "I do remember. Mrs. Ramirez made us get out a thesaurus and everything so our words wouldn't be 'basic.'" They both laughed and then Bennett added softly, "Caroline Marie Roland."

"Nope, just doesn't sound as good as Bennett Ryan Williams. Mine *is* too basic." She looked over to him as she twisted a loose piece of hair back into her bun. "Do you remember what you put on my paper?"

Bennett nervously stirred in his seat. "Oh, um, I mean—" he chuckled as he picked his coffee up to take a sip, but set it down when he realized it was empty.

"Don't worry, Bennett," Caroline said as she rolled her eyes. "I don't remember either." She smiled at him, deciding to let him go on this one even though she did remember exactly what she had put on his paper. *Benevolent. Receptive. Winsome.* The only reason she even remembered the words was because she probably never used them to describe anyone again. To be completely honest, she probably never used those words again period.

She began to think about the other things they could have conversations about. She didn't want to bring up college. She didn't particularly want to bring up their dead family members. She could've talked about....

"So, editor of the yearbook, huh?"

Bennett beat her to it. She didn't mind that much, though. She definitely could've talked for ages about the yearbook. "Yes," she said with another smile. Her cheeks were beginning to twitch.... "It's been amazing. I've been working with a few others to decide on the theme this year, but nothing sticks. It's due in about three months—they want to have it ready before senior skip week in May—but I can't seem to decide what I want this year to represent."

"I'm sure you'll figure out something. You always do. Didn't you come up with the theme for my senior yearbook?"

He remembered. "I did."

"I really liked that one. Wasn't it 'It Only Gets Better'?"

She smiled widely. "Yeah, I really liked that one, too."

"I heard you had a huge part in making that whole thing. The section for seniors where you put what they wanted to go for and who they wanted to be under each picture? That had to be my favorite part. It kind of made everyone more real if that makes sense."

It did make sense. It was the whole reason she wanted to do that theme. "Exactly. That one was amazing so how in the world am I supposed to top that for my own senior yearbook? I gave you the good one," she pouted. She realized then how closely they were leaning into each other. They had closed almost the entire distance between them as they had talked. It suddenly made her very aware of everything that was him. Caroline saw the dimple in his right cheek as he smiled. She saw how brown his eyes were. She could smell the woodsy cologne that he had on. His skin matched the color of her coffee.

Her phone buzzed beside her. Caroline sat back, trying to clear her brain. "I better get going," she said with a smile. She looked down at her phone to see the four texts from Izzy. "My grandparents are going to be wondering where I am. Not to mention, Izzy won't stop blowing up my phone." She grabbed her bag and stood up.

"Wait," Bennett said a little loudly. He cleared his throat. "I'm staying here for a while until the fall semester. Would you wanna maybe do this again sometime?"

Caroline smiled softly, nodding, and grabbed his phone. His lock screen was literally a landscape and she shook her head.

"What?" he said with a laugh.

"Just unlock your phone, Bennett." She rolled her eyes at him.

He unlocked it quickly and handed it back to her. She went to the contacts app and typed in her name, number, and even address for good measure.

"This Friday I'm free," she said as she handed the phone back to him.

He looked down at her contact information and smiled. "This Friday," he parroted.

"Pick me up?"

"Sure," he nodded. "What do you want to go do?"

She looked down at him as he sat in his chair, coffee cup empty in front of him. She grabbed both of their cups to bring them back to the counter. "Surprise me," she smirked as she walked to the counter. She gave the cups to the barista and smiled.

As she began to walk out the door, she turned around to look at Bennett again. He was staring down at his phone, still smiling.

"Hey, Bennett?" she called.

His head jerked up and he looked at her, embarrassment lining his features.

"I really had a great time today," she said, holding the handle of the door.

"Me too," he replied.

Then she left, the bell dinging above her and a smile—so wide that it hurt—plastered on her face.

Chapter 4

Izzy had insisted that Caroline went to talk to her before she went home to her grandparents'. Caroline, of course, could not deter Izzy, and relented easily.

"Fine," she had said into her phone. "But only for a little while!"

So she and Izzy sat outside on the porch at Izzy's house as Izzy's parents cooked inside. Caroline could smell the empanadas, the cheese, everything. It made her stomach growl.

"So?" Izzy said, dragging the word out. "How was it? What happened? What did you guys even talk about?" Izzy was practically bouncing in her chair. She had always known about Caroline's crush on Bennett, but once he had moved away, Izzy dropped it because Caroline and Bennett never kept in touch.

"Slow down, Iz," Caroline laughed. "It was... amazing."

Izzy squealed and Caroline's hands flew up to her ears. "Did you guys kiss? He's a great kisser, I just know it."

"Izzy, this is the first time I've seen the guy in two years," Caroline said as her face scrunched up in amusement.

Izzy waved her hand at Caroline, shushing her. "That doesn't even matter. You guys have something together. You always have."

Caroline rolled her eyes but on the inside she only felt warm and fuzzy. "Well, anyway, we talked about yearbook, and the classes we used to have in school. He told me that he just finished an internship, so he'll be hanging around until the fall semester."

"Oh my gosh, that's even better!" Izzy said.

"He's still going back to Massachusetts, Iz. It's not like long-distance relationships work anyway." As soon as it came out of her mouth, Caroline knew it was the wrong thing to say. "I didn't mean—I mean, it wasn't about—"

Izzy looked sad then, but just shook her head. "No, I know what you meant."

"Hey, girls, supper is ready." Izzy's mom poked her head out the front door.

"I actually can't stay, Mrs. Mendoza. My grandparents are expecting me." Caroline stood up and gave Izzy's mom a hug before turning around to hug Izzy as well. She whispered, "I'm sorry," into her friend's ear.

Izzy whispered, "I know, Caro," as she stood up too and pointed a finger at Caroline. "You better keep me updated," she said loudly.

Caroline laughed as she walked down the front steps of the porch. "Of course, Iz."

***

When Caroline arrived back at her grandparents' house, she knew that they would have already eaten supper and were most likely getting ready for bed. That's why when Caroline saw her grandfather sitting at the kitchen table, she nearly fell over in surprise.

"Jeez, Gramps, you scared the heck out of me," Caroline said as she held her hand to her chest.

He laughed heartily and said, "I am allowed to be in the kitchen of my own house."

Caroline rolled her eyes and smiled at him. "Of course," she said as she leaned down to kiss him on the cheek. Something was sitting on his lap and Caroline gave him a questioning look.

Caroline's heart nearly stopped when her gramps pulled the envelope from his lap and laid it on the table. It was the mail. She had forgotten to get the damn mail, and the huge white envelope on the table was proof. It was from the office of admissions at Florida State University....

Suddenly, Caroline felt as if she couldn't breathe. The air was stale. The room was hot. Everything around her became smaller and smaller and smaller.

"This came in for you today," he started. "It looks promising." Gramps handed her the large envelope. His small smile nearly broke her heart. He was tip-toeing around her—testing the waters—and Caroline absolutely hated that he had to do that.

She gingerly took the envelope from him, staring down at her hands as if they were on fire. Her eyes were wide and she began chewing on the inside of her lip to keep herself from hyperventilating.

"Caroline?"

She looked up, taken out of her trance. "Yes?"

"Are you okay?"

She could hear how genuine the question was in his voice. For a moment, she thought about breaking down right there in front of him. She thought about telling him everything. She thought about the pressure in her chest that never went away. The thoughts in her mind that never let her sleep. The constant fear that rippled through her at unexpected moments. But she couldn't tell him. She could hardly even open her mouth to breathe.

"I'm fine," she croaked. She cleared her throat and offered him a smile, never meeting his eyes. "Really." The smile, at least, made what she was saying a little more believable. "I'm gonna take this upstairs," she said, still staring down at the envelope.

"Will you let me know how it goes in the morning?" he asked.

"Of course," she told him, still not looking at him directly.

"I love you, kiddo," he smiled, his whole forehead crinkling with his eyes.

"I love you, too, Gramps," Caroline said as she finally met his gaze. It only shot lightning bolts through her chest, though, and made her stomach twist in knots.

Caroline turned away quickly and hurried back to her room. She paced back and forth when the door was closed, the envelope resting on her desk. She couldn't bring herself to sit down. She couldn't make herself *calm* down.

Her breathing picked up as she grabbed the envelope from her desk, pacing once more. She flipped it around in the palms of her hands. Her lungs seized up as she took one staggering breath in. Caroline sank down to the floor, resting her back against the wall. She stared down at the envelope. At the college she had dreamed about since she was a child. She stared down at what she wanted her future to be. Inhale.

One. Two. Three. Four.

Caroline's heart felt as if it was going to beat right out of her chest. She sliced the envelope open and pulled several papers out. As she turned the papers around, she saw pictures of campus—happy students as they sat on the quad. When she saw the first paper in the pile, it was a single, white piece with three paragraphs on it.

Dear Caroline Roland,
Congratulations! You have been accepted into
Florida State University....

Slapping the papers face down on the floor, Caroline started to rub the back of her neck and concentrated on her breathing. She was shutting her eyes tightly, grabbing fistfuls of hair and pulling, feeling her airways closing off. The pressure in her chest was unbearable.

No. That wasn't what she wanted. It had been so much easier thinking that she just didn't get in. Why had she sent her application out? Why had she kept doing that to herself? College after college. Letter after letter.

She opened her eyes and saw the pictures of campus again. She pulled her cardigan up to her mouth and screamed into it until her throat felt raw and papery.

Caroline stood abruptly, throwing the empty envelope in the trashcan. She held the acceptance letter in her hands, feeling the weight of everything that came with it. Then, she opened the bottom right drawer of her desk. She looked down at six other letters. Six other campuses. Six other *congratulations!*

Her face contorted into an ugly scowl. She felt her body beginning to tremble as she threw the letter and the campus and the congratulations into the drawer with the rest of them. She sat down in the chair at her desk, putting her head in her hands. She took several deep breaths and looked up at the letter tacked to her cork board.

Dear Caroline Roland,
Congratulations! You have been accepted into
Arizona State Community College....

As she stared up at the only acceptance letter that she could bear, she tried to think about the good things. She would be able to work at the pharmacy fulltime in college. She got to stay close to Gramps and Grams. She wouldn't have to worry about that pressure in her chest with them around and no college decisions to be made. Everything would go back to normal. She would be normal again. If she could just start college. If she could just put FSU behind her.

All she could hear in her head was *congratulations congratulations congratulations.* It repeated over and over again along with *FSU Mom FSU Mom FSU.... It's what she would've wanted....*

Caroline opened her laptop and navigated to FSU's website. She looked at dormitories. *Just be normal.* She saw campus maps. *Fix it.* Caroline looked at online tours. *What's wrong with you?*

It was what Mom would have wanted.
Fix it.

Just be normal, Caroline.
Congratulations.
She tried making a list:

<u>All the Reasons Why FSU Sucks:</u>

1.

She couldn't think of anything. Caroline felt something in her chest break as she gasped. It felt as if she were shattering, pieces of her fragmenting and becoming irreparable. Broken. Damaged. Her lungs would not move and her fingers and toes and lips began to tingle. She shut her eyes, praying for it to go away.

Breathe. Just breathe.

But she couldn't. She couldn't seem to suck in a breath. As soon as she began to breathe in, her lungs would quake and all she could do was exhale what little air she got in her lungs. She was going to die. She was sure of it.

Was this how her mom felt when her throat was closing?

Black spots colored her vision. Panic rose to the back of her throat, tasting sour. She grabbed at her throat: scratching, clawing, breaking the skin. Her breaths came in short gasps.

Caroline fell to the floor, the chair crashing loudly beside her.

Wheezing, whistling, rasping. She couldn't breathe. She couldn't make herself breathe. *Stop thinking about it.* If she stopped thinking about it, it would all go away. That was it: just stop thinking. Why couldn't she just fix it, damn it?!

She vaguely registered her grandparents coming into her room, kneeling down beside her, asking her what was wrong.

"I can't breathe," she gasped. "I can't breathe," she sobbed over and over and over again. Tears streamed down her cheeks as her chest painfully heaved, devastating sobs ripping from her throat.

It's what she would have wanted.

Congratulations… congratulations… congratulations.

Just stop thinking.

Just stop.

Breathe.

Chapter 5

She didn't leave the house after that. Not for school. Not for yearbook. Not for anything. Well, except her mandated therapy sessions. She didn't even want to step foot outside in fear of breaking again and somehow therapy always made her feel like she was going to break even more. It wasn't like she had many pieces left to break anyway, though.

Last Saturday wasn't the first time that had happened. It was at least the eighth time since her mother.... The first time was a week after her mother's death. After that, she began going to therapy. She could hide the panic then. She was able to confine it to the inside of her car; anytime she felt the panic, she would wait there until it passed. She always felt like she was going to die. She hadn't died yet though.

It wasn't like she had talked to Dr. B about any of that. She hadn't gotten better. She had just gotten better at hiding it. She had hid it so well for six months, had kept her panic to herself. After last Saturday night, her grandparents knew that, too. There was no hiding it after that.

It was Friday and Caroline had just gotten dropped off at Dr. B's office. She stared at the yellow walls, but they morphed into smoking black charcoal before her eyes. The yellow couldn't hide everything underneath.

"Caroline, you have to talk to me," Dr. B said, exasperation littering her tone.

Caroline couldn't. She had barely talked to anyone all week except to say "yes," "no," and "thank you." Not to her grandparents. Not to Izzy. Especially not to Dr. B.

"What you went through, Caroline, it—"

"I know what I went through!" Caroline felt the heat crawling up to her cheeks. Not from embarrassment, though. It was white, hot rage. "I don't need to relive it every damn day that I've come here this week." Caroline's hands were shaking. She began wringing them together in her lap, trying to get the nervous energy to leave her body.

Dr. B took in a deep breath and nodded. Caroline was surprised at that. She didn't think Dr. B would agree with her. "I'm not trying to make you relive it," she started. "I'm trying to make you *understand* it."

Nope. It definitely wasn't agreement. Just a nod to let Caroline know that she had heard her. She wasn't going to talk to Dr. B anymore. She knew what she went through. She understood why it happened. It had happened because Caroline was trapped in Valor City, Arizona. She wasn't trapped by her grandparents—they wanted her to go to FSU. She wasn't trapped by college acceptances. She wasn't even trapped by funding. She was trapped by her own damned mind and that was the worst part about it. How could she want something so badly, but her mind still limited her to her own backyard?

After her time was up, Dr. B excused her and Caroline politely murmured a "thank you" as she left. Her grams was waiting for her in the parking lot. She wasn't even allowed to drive herself around.

"How was it?" Grams asked her.

Yes. No, that wasn't the correct response. "Fine, thank you." Caroline was staring down at her phone, sorting the colors into vials. She held back her rage and her pain and her heavy chest. Instead of letting all of those emotions out, she just held them in like she always did, chewing on her lip until she tasted blood.

Grams stayed parked in the parking lot of Dr. B's office. "Did she fill you a prescription for a different medication? The one you have now obviously isn't working."

That made Caroline jerk in her seat. "I don't need a prescription, Grams. I'm not sick." Had Grams *asked* Dr. B to give her a new prescription?

Grams held up her hands in surrender. All Caroline could do was think about all the side effects. Everything about the medicine they already had her on Caroline had researched and read and analyzed the side effects. They couldn't blame her if they found out that she wasn't taking them, could they?

"You have to talk to us, sweetie. We can't help if we don't know why you're hurting. What caused you to feel so... out of control on Saturday?"

Out of control. Grams had to think a lot before choosing those words, Caroline knew that much. Caroline thought about finally confessing to what bothered her most: that she couldn't be alone. She didn't want to be like her mother, dying all by herself with no one around. She didn't want to move away and become more alone than she had ever been in her life. The isolation was suffocating. Knowing that her mother wanted her to go to FSU and knowing that her mother also died alone with no one to help her contradicted every thought Caroline ever had those days. Leave? She couldn't. The overwhelming fear and darkness prevented her from going further than her hometown by herself. Stay? She couldn't. Then she would be letting her mom down. She would be breaking a promise that she had made to herself all those years ago, and God knew she had done enough to let her mother down.

So, that was the turning point. Confess to all her fears, tell her Grams she got accepted into FSU, and dealing with the consequences were all part of that confession. She'd have to tell them about her mother. About that night.... Or, she could keep it to herself. Work it out on her own. Not be forced into a decision just because her grandparents knew she was afraid and that she wouldn't make the decision herself.

"I didn't get into FSU," she heard herself saying. A blatant lie, but somehow it sounded so believable and broken coming out of her mouth.

Her gram's face crumbled. "Oh, honey," she said as she pulled Caroline into a hug. Caroline let the tears come because she knew that was one of the only acceptable moments she would have to cry for a long time. After that—after outright lying to her grandmother—Caroline would have to become better than ever at hiding her emotions. She would have to act like she accepted the fact that she did—didn't—get into FSU.

"You can always try again next year and transfer," her grandmother told her, pulling away from the hug.

Caroline wiped away her tears and smiled hopefully, playing her part well. She nodded, sniffling instead of speaking. It was time for her to build her life around her lie. There was no going back. The decision was made.

***

"We'll be right back," Gramps said to her as he kissed the top of her head. Caroline felt her insides twist as she thought about being so alone in that house. "I'm just gonna help your grams with the groceries. Thirty minutes tops."

Caroline smiled and nodded, trying to act as if it were okay. But it wasn't. She wasn't sure if she could handle being alone just yet. Not so soon after what had happened Saturday. She let them go anyway, though, knowing that thirty minutes couldn't last that long. It was far better waiting thirty minutes by herself than letting them see the absolute mess she still was.

Not even ten minutes after they had left, the doorbell rang. Caroline walked cautiously to the front door, feeling her heart as it skipped a beat, and looked out the peephole.

It was Bennett. *Holy shit*, it was Bennett. How had he...? Then she remembered giving him her number and her address. She remembered telling him that she was free on Friday for a date. Caroline looked down at herself then back through the peephole.

Should she just ignore it?

He rang the doorbell again and Caroline jumped.

She quickly opened the door and looked out at him. He jerked back, surprised at her quick arrival.

"Oh, sorry," he said, referencing towards the doorbell.

She shook her head. "I—" she started, but couldn't find the words.

"You did tell me Friday, right? Because I'm totally horrible with dates—I mean not like *date* dates, but, you know, dates like the time like—"

"Bennett," she exhaled, interrupting him with the first smile she had felt all week. "Yes, I did tell you Friday, I just.... I wasn't really prepared to—"

"Yeah, I'm sorry, I had tried texting and calling but I didn't get an answer, so I wasn't sure if you had typed it in wrong or something had happened or—" he stopped himself abruptly, looking into her eyes with an apologetic smile. "I'm sorry if this is weird. You know, me showing up at your house. You not responding to my texts and calls." He was reaching up to rub the back of his neck, but Caroline quickly, softly grabbed his hand.

"I gave you my number for a reason, Bennett. I gave you my address for a reason. I *did* want to go on a date with you. Something just happened recently and I haven't been myself lately. I completely forgot and my phone has kind of been on airplane mode, I'm so sorry."

He looked down at their hands and let out an audible sigh of relief. "No, it's completely fine. I'm just glad you weren't—" he cleared his throat. "It's fine. Airplane mode, huh?"

Caroline rubbed her thumb over his hand ever so slightly before releasing it. She felt... alive. Electric in a way that she had never felt before. She looked down at her own hands, wondering if she had touched a live wire.

"Yeah, I was just trying to drown out the noise. If that makes any sense at all." Caroline twisted her hands together in front of her, feeling awkward for admitting to that.

"It makes complete sense," he said, nodding softly.

They stood there in silence for a long moment, neither of them daring to speak.

"I'll just head home then," he said awkwardly, pointing to his parked car behind him.

"No," she said as she shook her head. "I—I'm not ready to go out, but maybe—I mean, if you're okay with it—we could stay in? Watch a movie? My grandparents will be home in about ten or twenty minutes, but they won't mind."

Bennett's smile almost covered his whole entire face. "I'd like that."

So, Bennett came inside, sat on the couch, and scrolled through movies on the streaming service that Caroline had as she made popcorn. She watched the microwave and the bag of popcorn as it *pop pop popped*. Caroline thought about how easy it was to forget about everything when Bennett was around. She didn't have to think about the darkness. She didn't have to worry.

That's when she thought of it: Bennett could be her distraction. Not in a way that she would lead him on, just that he would.... He could help her forget for a while until it was too late to send FSU her decision. She could lean on him. He could be her support. May 1st. She only had to forget until then. Then, she could be honest with everyone, honest with Bennett. He was only staying until the fall anyway, so it wasn't like they would turn into something more. He would just be around for her. She liked having him around, liked his company. It was easy around him. He was easy to lean into.

Caroline took the bag of popcorn out without waiting for the microwave to ding. She put the popcorn in a bowl and brought it out to meet Bennett. "Found anything good?" she asked as she sat down beside him.

"I wasn't sure what genre you'd want to watch," he said, smiling sheepishly.

She smiled down at her lap. It could work. Having him around could work. It *would* work. He was so sweet, so kind. "Maybe one of those doomsday films? You know, the ones where the world is always ending and the characters have to find some way to survive?"

Bennett laughed. "That works," he said.

"Caroline?"

She turned to see her grams and gramps walking in the door, a handful of groceries in each of their arms. She jumped to her feet to go help them. Bennett did the same.

Her grandparents looked at Bennett with raised eyebrows.

"Grams, Gramps," Caroline started, "this is Bennett. He came over to keep me company."

They both looked at him with gracious smiles as he took the groceries from their arms. "It's very nice to meet the two of you," he said.

"And you, too," Grams said, smiling at Bennett but then turned to Caroline and gave her a secret smile. "Are you from here, Bennett?"

"Born and raised," Bennett replied easily.

"So, you went to high school with Caroline?" Gramps chimed in.

"Yes," Bennett said, beginning to blush slightly. "I'm in college now." Gramps raised his eyebrows slightly and Bennett tripped over a few of his words. "We're only two years apart," he said, and it made Caroline smile to see him flustered like that.

Gramps laughed and patted Bennett on the back as Bennett let out a sigh of relief.

They all put up the groceries in relative silence after that with a few more questions about Bennett's personal life. When they were done, Caroline kissed her Grams and Gramps on the cheek as they told her goodnight. Grams went up to Bennett and told him how nice it was to meet him while also telling him thank you—Caroline thought—for more than just the groceries. Grams and Gramps went to sleep after that.

"Thank you for, you know, helping out and everything," Caroline said as she and Bennett sat back down on the couch, closer than before.

"It really isn't a big deal. Just the polite thing to do." Bennett shrugged it off as if it meant nothing. It meant everything to Caroline.

"You know, it's not every day you meet a guy willing to unload the groceries," Caroline said nonchalantly.

Bennett laughed and Caroline wanted to hear it over and over and over again. So, she tried to be funny for him, and he didn't have to do hardly anything at all to make her forget about the darkness.

He just had to be there with her—*for* her—and it all went away. She could make it to decision day if she had Bennett around. She could keep telling her lies for just a few more months, and then everything would be okay. The darkness would be gone. She would be able to breathe again.

In the end, they finished eating the popcorn before they ever picked a movie.

Chapter 6

It was time for Caroline to go back to school. Back to work. Back to her life. She got the weekend to prepare herself for it, but it still wasn't enough. It was early Monday morning—too early to even start getting ready for school. So, she had decided to finally face the noise.

When she turned her phone back off of airplane mode, she saw a barrage of text messages from Izzy, the ones from Bennett that he had told her about on Friday, and then one more from him. One a little more recent than the other ones.

SUN – 4:23PM

Bennett: Maybe we could watch that disaster movie soon?

Caroline smiled to herself, trying to think of a witty response that would make Bennett smile, too.

MON – 5:12AM

Caroline: Oh, yeah, the one we totally stood up Friday night?

Surprisingly, Bennett texted back almost immediately.

Bennett: I'm just glad it wasn't me....

Caroline laughed. She technically *had* stood him up, but she felt like she had made up for it by inviting him inside. Not to mention that they had talked for hours after that, totally ignoring the movie they had chosen. They had never even pressed play.

Caroline thought about what she had to do that day. School until noon, pick up the mail (even though she wasn't even sure why she was bothering anymore), work at the pharmacy.... She thought about work. Grams and Gramps had told her that Curtis was leaving early that day from work, so she'd be alone for a few hours at the pharmacy. She had somehow convinced them that she was gonna be okay and that they didn't need to babysit her, but now she had to figure out a way to actually make it *be* okay. Earlier, she had thought about asking Izzy to go with her to work, but Caroline thought that if Bennett was available, she might be able to get him to go meet her instead.

After her plan was solidified in her mind, Caroline began to look at Izzy's text messages.

SUN – 11:16 AM
Izzy: How're things with Bennetttt??

MON – 8:20 AM

Izzy: C'mon, Caro, it can't be bad enough to skip class.

Izzy: Or are things too good??

MON – 6:17 PM

Izzy: Where are you?

TUE – 12:10 PM

Izzy: Caroline can you please answer me?

TUE – 4:23 PM

Izzy: Caroline??

TUE – 8:42 PM

Izzy: I called your gramps and grams. I don't know what happened, but can you please call me? I won't ask questions, I just wanna know you're okay.

FRI – 2:52 PM

Izzy: Like I said, I'm not asking any questions. I know you hate talking about stuff like this.

Izzy: Buuuttt I have all your homework, notes for classes, and even a Pop-Tart from the concession stand waiting for you when you finalllllyy decide to answer me.

Caroline immediately felt bad for turning her phone on airplane mode. Not only had she stood up Bennett, but she had ignored her best friend. It had always felt difficult to Caroline to talk about what was going on when she was trapped in her own mind by her own thoughts. She had tried to tell Izzy about it once, but almost did exactly what she had done last Saturday. Talking about it just made her throat swell until it felt like she couldn't breathe. So, that was why it hurt her even more to see how caring and kind Izzy was in all of her texts.

MON – 5:25 AM

Caroline: Can I have that Pop-Tart today?

Immediately, a response came back.

Izzy: Sorry, offer expired.
Izzy: ....
Izzy: And I ate it......
Izzy: But I'll get you a new one if you come to school today!!
Caroline: Lunch date?
Izzy: Lunch date.

Caroline thought then about her best friend and all the ways Izzy had helped her through things that were less than pleasant. Izzy had been there for all of the hard parts. Each point in Caroline's life that she thought she couldn't get any lower. When Caroline and her mom had first moved to Arizona after her dad had died, Izzy was there for her. It was what started their strong friendship. It was what made Izzy the best. She had been there when Caroline's mom had died. So, why couldn't Caroline open up about her feelings when Izzy had already seen the ugliest of those emotions before?

She decided to stop thinking about the darkness. She didn't want to waste any more time on it that morning. So instead, she began getting ready for the day. Since it was so early, Caroline thought she might as well make herself more presentable than usual. She chose an outfit that fit her well, paired with a long, over-sized cardigan. She let her hair flow loose around her shoulders and down her back, running an anti-frizz cream through the ends. Once she finished her makeup, she picked out a dainty gold necklace with a heartbeat on it and put in gold studs for earrings.

Caroline felt more put together than she had in a while. Look confident, feel confident she guessed.

She sent Bennett a text asking if he wanted to hang out with her while she worked. She knew he'd say yes before she even got the confirmation text.

Izzy texted her again at six thirty and asked Caroline if she wanted a ride. Caroline couldn't have been happier to accept. Even though her grandparents had withheld her driving privileges since Saturday, she felt like she needed the company on her first day back at school. Even if Izzy drove like a crazy person.

Once Izzy showed up in front of her house, Caroline kissed her grams and gramps goodbye before walking out the door.

"Caroline!" Izzy basically screamed as soon as Caroline opened the door.

She almost fell to the concrete from how loud Izzy had yelled. Caroline grabbed at her chest and let out a breath as she sat down in the car.

"I've got so much to tell you, but first, thank *God* you're back. Like, school just isn't the same and I know we only have half days, but they're so long without you there."

Caroline laughed. "I've missed you too, Iz."

Izzy began driving and her words came out as fast as her car was going. "Okay, first off. Are you okay? Is it contagious? Or was it Bennett? Do I need to kick his ass?"

Caroline subtly grabbed what her Gramps coined the "Oh Shit" handle as Izzy swerved around a piece of trash in the road. "Definitely not contagious, and it was not Bennett. He's still amazing."

Izzy's eyebrows rose. "You've seen him recently?"

Caroline pulled at some frays in her jeans. "Friday...."

"So, you've been ignoring me, but you could easily talk to him?" Izzy joked as she gave Caroline a condescending look.

She laughed—she couldn't help it—because Izzy was so easygoing and hardly ever got mad about anything. "He's gonna meet me today while I work at the pharmacy."

Izzy squealed and Caroline snorted at her friend's ridiculousness. She loved the support, though. The unwavering, unconditional support. "Speaking of boyfriends—"

"He's not my boyfriend, Iz—"

Izzy waved and shushed her. "Besides the point...." Izzy's face contorted into an smile that Caroline almost needed sunglasses for.

"*Tell me,*" Caroline prompted as Izzy looked as if she was going to burst.

"Nick told me he loves me...."

"Oh. My. God." Caroline said slowly. Then, she and Izzy's eyes met as they shrieked together. Izzy had just parked in the school parking lot. Caroline shoved her arm. "So, what did you say back?"

"That I love him, of course!" Izzy yelled and Caroline reached over the seat to hug her best friend. "And I got accepted at SCU!"

Caroline had to bring the excitement back to her face because the mention of colleges caught her off guard. "What the actual heck, Iz! How is it possible to miss this much in a week?" She reached back over to give her friend another hug. "I'm so happy for you."

"What about you?" Izzy said as she pulled away. "Have you heard anything from FSU?"

Caroline shook her head. "You know I'm going to Arizona State Community College, Iz."

Izzy shrugged. "I mean, I know you *said* you were going there, but I didn't think you *meant* it. You had always talked so much about FSU and I just thought that you were worried you wouldn't get in, I mean—"

"I didn't get in," Caroline said. She might as well tell Izzy the lie now.

Izzy made a face. Caroline wasn't sure if she liked the suspicion that was lining her friend's face. Maybe the devastation wasn't convincing?

"How?" Izzy shook her head. "You literally have better grades than me."

"I don't know, I guess I just didn't do enough senior year. Maybe they wanted someone who was more well-rounded." Caroline knew as soon as it left her mouth that it was the wrong thing to say.

"*Well-rounded*?" Izzy said, baffled.

"Can we just not talk about it?" Caroline hurriedly said. "I just—I don't want to talk about it anymore."

Izzy shook her head again, the surprise still not leaving her face. "I'm sorry, Caro."

Caroline waved her off. "Let's just go inside."

***

Caroline had the SD card from her camera in the computer as she watched the progress of her upload. She was in yearbook class for her last class of the day. It was mostly seniors, but there were still a few juniors, sophomores, and freshmen. It was in a computer lab and each student had their job of uploading pictures from school functions and editing them to adjust lighting, contrast, exposure, and other things. Their teacher, Mr. Johnson, had been a freelance photographer for most of his life, so he taught them all about the settings on their cameras as well as what to do with the pictures once you had them uploaded onto the computer.

"Caroline," he said as he came up behind her. "It's good to have you back. Have you thought a little more about the theme for the yearbook?"

Caroline turned in her seat to face him. "No, sir, but I'm sure we'll come up with something soon."

He smiled down at her, "In the end, Caroline, it's your choice for what you want the theme to be. Just remember that."

She nodded as his face drifted to her screen. The picture that she was editing was of Izzy doing her "athlete" pose.

"That one's great," he said with a laugh.

Caroline turned back to her screen. "Yeah, I like it too," she smiled.

He left to go see another student's progress as Caroline moved on to the next photo she needed to edit. It was the one of Bennett. He was caught off guard, his glasses falling off his nose, coffee-colored skin catching the sun. His eyes were closed as he laughed, and Caroline wanted to reach out to touch him through the screen.

Her trance was broken by the sound of a keyboard being typed on a little aggressively. She looked over to see a freshman hitting keys roughly, murmuring things like "C'mon, work!" He had a baby face and looked much younger than Caroline thought a freshman should look.

As she stood up, she walked over to him to see that he was trying to edit one of his pictures. "That's a good picture," she said over his shoulder. It was from a baseball game. The batter had just swung at the ball, connecting with it as it sailed towards the edge of the picture. The settings were done in such a way that when the picture was taken, the sunlight had lit up just the batter's box. It really was a great shot.

"Yeah, the picture is fine, I just can never get this stupid editing program to work," he said, frustrated, as he hit another key on his keyboard angrily.

"What are you trying to do?" she asked.

"I'm just trying to adjust the lighting without blurring out the entire picture. I want the details to show but the light just screws it up."

"Try this," Caroline said as she showed him how to adjust the exposure, contrast, shadows, and brightness. The mixture of the four helped the picture's lighting to work perfectly.

He looked up at her curiously. "Thank you," he said as if he wasn't sure why she had helped him.

She smiled politely and went back to her seat. Bennett's face looked back at her from the computer screen and the smile remained on her face for a few moments longer.

Chapter 7

<u>Reasons why being alone sucks:</u>

1. There's no one there to talk to.
2. The silence is way too loud.
3. I have to find ways to occupy myself without freaking out.
4. Mom died alone.
5. I'm terrified of dying alone, too.
6. See #5.
7. See #5 again because it's literally the worst.
8. When I'm alone, the darkness always wins.

After their last class period, Izzy drove them both to Caroline's house. They had stocked up on Pop-Tarts at the concession stand before they left and were planning on having a picnic outside the backyard at the state line.

When they got to the house, Caroline started her normal routine of pulling the mail out of the mailbox, taking her mail out, and putting the rest back in the mailbox. There one letter from a college she applied to in Washington, but she didn't really expect anything positive back. It was one of the higher tiers academically and she honestly only applied to see if she could get in.

As Caroline pulled the mail out, Izzy eyed her suspiciously. In hindsight, Caroline probably should've waited for Izzy to leave to get the mail, but she really couldn't risk her grandparents finding another acceptance letter. It was hard enough to convince them that she *wanted* to go to the community college let alone that she didn't get in anywhere else.

"What exactly are you doing?" Izzy asked as Caroline put the mail back in the mailbox.

"Oh, um, just getting my mail," Caroline replied, not meeting Izzy's eyes.

"Shouldn't you just get all of it for your Gramps?"

"You know, he really enjoys getting the mail. It's a thing for him." Caroline, of course, knew this was complete bullshit. In all actuality, she just didn't want her grandparents to get suspicious when she got the mail every day and never told them about anything that was for her.

Izzy's eyebrows rose on her face but she didn't say anything. When they got inside the house, they grabbed a blanket and made two glasses of milk. As Caroline was getting ready to go outside, she grabbed the college letter and told Izzy that she was gonna run up to her room.

"I'll come with you," Izzy said as she put the blanket on the table with the Pop-Tarts and milk. "I've gotta put your red top up anyway."

Caroline couldn't exactly protest, and she had completely forgotten about the top Izzy had borrowed for Valentine's Day. So, she let Izzy follow her up to her room. As Izzy went into Caroline's closet to put the top up, Caroline hurriedly ripped open the college letter and read the first line.

Dear Caroline Roland,
We regret to inform you that we cannot offer you admission into....

Somehow after all of the acceptances and all of the congratulations, this rejection came easier than all of the others. Caroline breathed out a sigh of relief just as Izzy came up behind her.

"What did it say?" she asked.

Caroline showed her the letter, trying to hold back her enthusiasm from being rejected. "I didn't get in."

Izzy merely shrugged. "That's okay, Caro. That school is super hard to get into anyway. I think only one person from our high school has ever gotten in."

Caroline nodded in this weird mixture of solemnity and enthusiasm. She wasn't sure how to separate the two and she never was good at acting. So, she opened up her bottom right drawer to her desk and threw the letter in, closing it quickly so Izzy couldn't see the rest of the contents of the drawer.

Izzy and Caroline made their way back down to the kitchen and gathered their supplies. They went out to the backyard, opened the gate, and laid their blanket down on the state line. Izzy sat down first, taking her glass of milk from Caroline, and opened up the three different flavors of Pop-Tarts, spreading them out in a social media-worthy scene. Caroline couldn't help but to take a picture with her cell phone, hoping she could include it in the yearbook.

"I just love Utah," Izzy said as she broke a piece off of one of the fruity Pop-Tarts. Caroline always went for the chocolatey ones first.

"Definitely my favorite vacation spot," Caroline added, knowing that it was one of the truest statements she'd said in a long time.

***

After lunch, Caroline headed over to the pharmacy to work. Curtis was going to be there for the first two hours of her shift, and then after that Bennett had said he'd come visit her. So, she had all the time accounted for so that she wouldn't be alone at all.

As Caroline walked into the pharmacy, she saw Curtis at the front desk reading something. "Whatcha reading?" Caroline asked as she went up to him.

He held it up without saying a word. It was a manual for becoming a movie critic.

"Zen day?" Caroline asked with a slight smile creeping up the edge of her face.

Curtis nodded and Caroline slipped to the back, clocking in, and getting her pharmacy vest. Zen days, for Curtis at least, were quiet days when he needed to focus on his "craft." Sometimes he would break the silence and talk to her, but mainly Caroline thought it was because he just didn't want to speak to anyone. She wished she could do that. Being in therapy made it almost impossible.

Caroline began packaging pills with their warnings, their little white paper bags, and the information for the people taking the pills stuck to the front of the bag. She eventually got to a pill that caught her eye. It was the exact type of medicine that she was being prescribed. Caroline stared at the little white pills in their orange bottle and read the warning label.

May cause: dizziness, drowsiness, headaches, and in severe cases, memory loss, depression, and loss of concentration.

She didn't understand pills. One of the reasons she had wanted to become a pharmacist in the first place was to help people just like her grandfather did. Her reason for wanting to become a pharmacist so badly now was to make medicine that didn't cause so many side effects. How were drugs that could make you worse helping people? How could someone want her to take something that could make her worse?

Caroline put her head in her hands and sighed heavily. She just wanted to go home and take a nap. She wanted it to be May 1ˢᵗ so she could stop thinking about college and stop thinking about all of the things holding her back.

"Caroline?"

She jerked up in her seat to see Bennett in the doorway staring at her. "Bennett," she said, feeling shocked and confused. "I thought—"

"I wanted to surprise you and come a little earlier. Are you okay?" Bennett asked as he pushed his black-rimmed glasses up the bridge of his nose.

"Oh, yeah, just tired, you know," Caroline mumbled softly.

As if answering all of her prayers, Bennett held up a coffee. Caroline's expression immediately broke out into a smile—she couldn't help it. She laughed.

"Well don't you come prepared," she said, the laugh fading in her throat. She stood, hugged him, and grabbed the coffee from him, gesturing for him to take the seat next to her.

Bennett watched as she began working again. She read labels, packaged prescriptions, and moved back and forth from the back and the front of the pharmacy to put the finished prescriptions in place by the last name of whoever was taking them.

"Do you read all the warning labels?" Bennett asked after a while.

Caroline was surprised. She didn't think he was watching that closely. She also had no idea what she would tell him. If she did tell him that she read the warning labels, he'd probably think she was crazy. But the problem was that he had already noticed. So she couldn't exactly just make up a lie. Not to mention she was terrible at lying.

"Yeah," she said and hoped he'd leave it at that.

"Because of your mom?"

Caroline kept her head down and tried to continue working. He must've heard one of the rumors that went around when her mother died. That a drug interaction caused her mother's heart to stop. In a way, it was partly true. Caroline just never wanted to correct people because she couldn't stomach talking about it anyway.

She started making a list in her head:

How to keep Bennett from asking questions:
1. Talk about safe stuff like yearbook.
2. Never mention Mom.

"What are you doing?" Bennett asked.

Caroline almost threw up her hands, but started laughing instead. "You like asking questions, huh?" she asked with a smile, making sure to let him know that she wasn't trying to be rude.

He blushed furiously and Caroline's smile grew.

"You just—" he started and shook his head. "Ever since we met in school I've wanted to know more about you. Now you're here and I just—" Bennett looked down at his hands as he trailed off. "I want to know you, but I don't want to scare you off. I'm not exactly good at talking to people most of the time."

Caroline felt her heart swell as he spoke. She understood how he felt. She knew what it felt like to want something, to make sure that you don't mess it up, to feel vulnerable around someone, to just *be* in another person's company while overanalyzing yourself. It was emotionally exhausting. She stood up quickly and went over to him to give him a hug.

"You're doing great, Bennett, and I promise you're not scaring me off. I'm not so good with people either, so I completely understand," Caroline said as she pulled away from him.

Bennett laughed. "You don't have to tell me what I want to hear. Everyone loves you at school."

Caroline folded her arms across her chest. "The only reason I'm popular at school is because of how I look," she said as she rolled her eyes. Then she got serious and added, "And because of my mom.... No one wants to exclude the girl with the... well, you know."

He looked at her seriously. "Caroline," he said. "You're popular because you're kind. It may have something to do with how you look and your mom, but when we were in school together you were nice to everyone. It didn't matter who they were. You didn't care that I was nerdy or that my brother was the athlete. You didn't ignore me like some other people did or would just be nice to me to get to know my brother. You were genuinely *nice*. You still are." Bennett laughed and threw his hands up in the air. "I mean, I've never met anyone who wants *everyone* to be happy."

Caroline was speechless. She wasn't sure if there was anything she could say that could even come close to topping what he had just told her.

"Caroline?"

That was the second time that day Caroline was surprised by someone coming to see her. It was her Gramps walking through the door, Curtis trailing behind him.

"Hey Gramps," Caroline started, trying to get the fog to clear from her head. She felt like she was underwater. "Bennett came to hang out."

Gramps smiled at Bennett and they shook each other's hands. As they did, Curtis met Caroline's eyes, his eyebrows raised. He nodded towards Bennett as if to signal something to Caroline, but she couldn't figure out what.

"Hello, sir," Bennett said.

"Good afternoon, Bennett." Gramps turned towards Caroline and smiled at her. "Curtis was just about to leave and I was thinking that it would be great for you to take the rest of the afternoon off."

That was when Curtis smiled and nodded again. Caroline finally understood because Curtis was probably the one who suggested the idea to Gramps.

Caroline blinked. "I mean, yeah, if you think it's okay, Gramps."

"I wouldn't offer if I didn't think you deserved it, kiddo," Gramps said as he patted her shoulder. "Get her to have fun, Bennett. She definitely doesn't get out enough."

Caroline opened her mouth and laughed. "I have *fun*," Caroline said as she gently pushed her Gramps on the shoulder.

His eyebrows raised and Curtis laughed behind him. Caroline couldn't believe these men. They were bent on embarrassing her in front of Bennett.

"You heard the man," Bennett smiled, but then quickly looked over his shoulder to Gramps and said, "I mean, sir."

Chapter 8

Caroline and Bennett were sitting in Bennett's car with the engine idling. Neither of them had any idea what something "fun" would be, but whatever it was—according to Gramps—Caroline didn't do enough of it.

"We could go hiking?" Bennett offered.

Caroline's nose crinkled. She wasn't sure if "hiking" would be her idea of fun, and by the looks of Bennett, he didn't think so either.

"Yeah, you're right," Bennett chuckled.

Caroline's stomach growled and answered all of their questions. "Maybe food would be fun?" she smiled.

Bennett laughed and put the car in drive. "There's a little food truck down Main Street. It has the best hot dogs, and I think you'd love it."

Caroline didn't mention to him that she knew exactly what he was talking about—it was a small town after all—and she didn't mention that she had already tried the hot dogs there. The fact that Bennett had said she'd love it was enough for her.

She could smell the grease as soon as they pulled up and parked as close as they could. Her stomach began growling again and she couldn't wait to eat. Bennett laughed when he saw her expression, but he was right, they really did have the best hot dogs around. Specifically, they were called Sonoran hot dogs. Caroline could remember when she and her mom first moved to Arizona and someone had to explain to them exactly what they were. The only way Caroline could think to describe it to someone else was that the hot dog wiener had bacon wrapped around it, was put into a special bun, and topped with loads of onions, tomatoes, and pinto beans. Caroline's favorite part, though, was putting the jalapeño salsa on top. The food truck that they were at wasn't the only place serving Sonoran hot dogs, though. They just happened to be the best.

Bennett went up to the food truck and ordered two hot dogs with fries on the side and two cokes. While he ordered, Caroline picked a picnic table for them, wrapping her cardigan tightly around her chest as a gust of wind blew around her. She shivered slightly just as Bennett came to sit down next to her.

He watched her shiver and—without a word—went to his car. Caroline eyed him suspiciously. She guessed maybe he had a jacket or something for her in his car. What he came back with made her laugh so deeply that she could feel it in her belly.

"You keep that in your car?" she laughed, holding her sides.

"What?" he asked, a smile taking over his features. "It's super useful. C'mon, I'll show you." Bennett took the large bundle in his arms and slipped his arms through the holes. It was a *huge* blanket, but a jacket, too. Caroline couldn't remember what they always advertised them as on TV, but she wouldn't deny that it looked super comfortable.

Bennett walked in a small circle around the picnic table, showing her his jacket-blanket. Caroline couldn't stop laughing but the happiness she felt in her chest finally felt like it was reflecting what she was showing on the outside.

"Give it to me already. I'm cold and convinced," Caroline rasped out, her throat feeling dry and frozen from all of the laughter.

She stood up and, instead of giving it to her, Bennett took it off and held it up, waiting for Caroline to stick her arms out so he could put it on her. She felt his arms and hands as he slid the huge thing onto her arms. It was warm and comfortable and somehow made her feel safer.

When Caroline turned around to face Bennett, he was staring down at her, blushing. She looked up to meet his eyes and offered him a small smile.

Bennett coughed a little as he broke eye contact. "It looks *way* better on you."

Caroline smiled as she sat back down to eat. Bennett sat across from her, opened the paper around her straw, and stuck the straw in her drink for her.

"Well aren't you a gentleman," she said, trying to suppress her grin for at least a moment.

He shrugged nonchalantly as he took a huge bite of his hot dog. Caroline followed suit and finally got her stomach to stop growling at her after a few bites. They ate like this in silence for a few minutes. Caroline was enjoying every minute of it because it had been so long since she had eaten a Sonoran hot dog. When she thought about it, the last time was probably with her mom, and that thought stole the smile from her face. Her thoughts only spiraled from there, and it became so loud in her head that she couldn't make it go away.

Just go away.

You're fine.

She just wanted it all to stop. *Just stop.* It was her mother's face that she saw around her. It was her mother's hands picking up the hot dog. Her mother's eyes staring back at her. Her mother who died alone. *You're alone.* Her mother who couldn't breathe. *I can't breathe.*

Caroline's hands began to shake as her breath came in raggedy. Her chest felt heavy and tight. Black spots danced at the corners of her vision. She reached for her phone, wanting to take out the color sorting app, wanting it all to *stop*.

One. Two. Three. Four.

"Hey," Bennett said as he reached for her hand. "Are you okay?"

She looked up to meet his eyes. They were deep brown like melting chocolate. Warm. Safe. Not her mother's. Bennett's.

Caroline took a deep breath in and plastered a smile on her face. "Yeah, wow. I don't know what happened there. I must've been really out of it." She looked down at the hot dog on its paper boat, but she couldn't stomach another bite. Her stomach had soured.

She took a sip of her coke to clear the huge lump in her throat that had formed. Caroline looked back up at Bennett and he was still studying her. He watched her as if she were broken and she couldn't take another second of it.

"I'm fine, Bennett. Really. Just kind of got lost in a thought," she said, shrugging as if those thoughts were not consuming her. As if they hadn't taken over her entire mind and body and soul.

"They must have been some really dark thoughts," he said, concern lining his features, but that wasn't what Caroline focused on. It was the small imperceptible nod that Bennett gave her. The one that said, "I understand," without speaking a single word. The one that told her that she didn't need to explain anything. He was there for her. He was there. She wasn't alone.

***

Bennett was driving her home, and somehow, it was already getting dark. He hadn't said much since Caroline's freak out, and she couldn't help thinking that she had scared him off. Overthinking everything happened to be Caroline's superpower.

"Do you remember my brother?" Bennett asked as he stared ahead at the road, his headlights growing brighter with the sun setting behind them.

"Josh, right?"

Bennett nodded. "Joshua."

"Wasn't he a senior when I was a freshman?"

Bennett nodded again and shared a sad smile with her. "He did everything. Football. Track. Student Council. Homecoming king. If you could describe who a golden child would be, it would be him."

He still wasn't looking at Caroline and she couldn't tell whether he was upset or sad or simply just telling her a story.

"And I know the way I'm saying all of this must make you think that I hated him, but I didn't." Bennett took in a deep breath and—for a second—Caroline was terrified that he was going to start crying. "We were only a year apart, so we were really close. At least, I mean, I think we were."

Bennett remained silent for a few moments more. Caroline couldn't imagine what he was going through. She knew how she felt losing her mom. At least her mother's death was an accident.

Bennett began speaking again, "He was the best brother. He never let me think that I was worth anything less than him even though I didn't accomplish half of the things that he did. He was so kind. Kind of like you, Caroline. He was nice to everyone, it didn't matter who they were.

"Anyway. The reason I'm saying this is because when I lost him, every memory I had with him was destroyed. They all became dark thoughts."

Caroline finally realized why he was talking about his brother.

"Everything became a question of why or why not. I know it hasn't been long since you lost your mom, but those dark thoughts will only get darker if you let them. I have to remember that even though Josh isn't here anymore, those memories were based on his kindness, on every good thing we did together. I know you're still hurting. I see it every time you look away into nothing. But you can't just let every good thing that ever happened with your mom turn dark."

She started shivering again, but it wasn't from the cold. "I don't want to talk about this, Bennett," she choked out. Her throat was feeling tight again.

"That's okay," he said. "I'll be here if you ever do want to talk about it."

"You make it sound easy," Caroline blurted out. She could hear the tears in her own voice. "To just forget and move on and act like they were never here."

"That's not what I'm saying. I never forget about Josh. Not one single day. I just smile now when I think of him instead of turning in on myself."

Caroline wanted to change the subject. He sounded like her therapist and she didn't want to talk to either of them at the moment. "You don't sound like a lawyer," she said to divert the attention from her. "You sound more like a therapist to me."

That was when Bennett's sad smile faltered, and Caroline felt horrible. He was just trying to help her. He wanted her to feel better and she was obviously not helping anyone in this situation, not even herself.

"I'm sorry, Bennett, I just—"

"No," he interrupted. "You're right. I have no room to be talking to you about this stuff. I still can't get over some of my own problems, so I'm the last one who should be helping you with yours." He pushed his glasses up the bridge of his nose and Caroline just wanted to hug him again.

"Bennett, I—" she started, feeling the tears crawling back up her throat to choke her. She coughed to try and make them go away, but it didn't work. "I've been so messed up since my mom died and I haven't been able to get anything to go back to normal." Her tears were threatening to overflow, but she knew if she let them come, she wouldn't be able to finish her thoughts. "All I've wanted is for everything to go back to the way it was, but it'll never be like that again. You know how that feels. I'm just—"

They pulled up in front of her grandparents' house and she decided to show him exactly what she was trying to say.

"C'mon," she said as she got out the car and gestured for him to get down with her.

When he came around to meet her, she grabbed his hand and led him to the backyard. They walked through the gate and out into the open space around her grandparents' house. Caroline found her spot and took a deep breath as she sat down. Bennett slowly sat down next to her.

"Can you guess where we are?" Caroline asked with a small smile.

"Your backyard?" Bennett squinted at her with an apologetic look as he shrugged.

"Utah. We are currently sitting on the state line entering into Utah."

Bennett looked beyond confused and Caroline couldn't blame him. She wasn't sure how exactly she had started this routine of coming out there to sit on the state line. She wasn't even sure how it made her feel better because most of the time, it only ever made her feel worse. All she knew at that moment was that she didn't want to talk about her mom, but she definitely didn't want to push Bennett away. She could feel that she was doing just that by not talking to him. He shared something with her. The least she could do was give him something small in return.

"The reason I come out here is because it feels like the furthest place from home I can get without breaking into pieces," Caroline started. She knew she wasn't making sense because Bennett hadn't said anything, so she tried to piece together something that he'd be able to understand.

"Being alone," she started, "isn't exactly something I'm good at doing. Every time I try to be alone—even when I know that someone I know isn't too far away—I start... panicking, I guess." Caroline stopped to take a breath, feeling like what she was saying was the most draining conversation she had ever had in her life. "So, when I come out here, I can convince myself that I'm fine. I can almost get it to where I'll believe that I can function like a normal human being because if I can go to another state and be alone, I should be able to do anything."

It stayed quiet for a long moment as Caroline stared out into the openness. There were so many stars that night that Caroline could almost smile. Instead, she felt the tears coming back behind her eyes. It was the never-ending story of her life. Smile on the outside. Be happy on the outside. Prove to everyone that she's fine on the outside. But, inside? Those smiles couldn't be further from the truth.

"My mother died alone," Caroline said suddenly. "That's kind of when this all started."

Bennett nodded, and Caroline knew he understood. Losing someone that close to you doesn't allow you to stay the same person you were before. She knew that, and so did he.

Bennett slowly reached over and grabbed her hand, holding it tight in his as she felt his warmth radiate into her. She scooted closer to him and laid her head on his shoulder. He rested his head against hers.

"Though my soul may set in darkness, it will rise in perfect light; I have loved the stars too truly to be fearful of the night," Bennett said, running circles on the back of her hand with his thumb. "It's from a poem by Sarah Williams."

"I didn't know lawyers quoted poetry," Caroline said finally letting the smile reach her lips, but Bennett tensed beside her, and she somehow knew it was the wrong thing to say.

Chapter 9

On Friday, Caroline felt exhausted before she ever even opened her eyes. She had stayed up almost all night—as she had been doing for most of the week—staring at the ceiling and going over the day that she had just had. She hadn't seen Bennett since Monday, but they had texted constantly. Caroline knew he was holding back on something, she just couldn't find out what. She wasn't exactly being one hundred percent truthful either, but it bothered her that she couldn't see what was hurting him. So, that's what plagued her thoughts every night as she stared at the ceiling. When her alarm would actually go off, she wouldn't even be sleeping, but in some weird half-awake half-asleep trance.

Caroline and Bennett had plans to see each other that night. It wasn't necessarily her idea but Izzy's. Izzy had planned a double date for her, Nick, Caroline, and Bennett, and Caroline couldn't exactly say no. It actually made her super anxious to go on a double date because Bennett and Caroline's dates hadn't exactly been official. That night would be official. And Caroline couldn't keep her nerves from going into overdrive.

She and Izzy had just walked into their homeroom together. Izzy was going on and on about the double date and Caroline thought if she wrung her hands together any more, it would cause her to bruise.

"Report cards are getting issued today," her homeroom teacher announced.

Chatter rose all around them as people's desks scraped across the floor. It all became a little too much for Caroline and she desperately wanted to pull out her phone to open the color sorting app. She couldn't, though, and she definitely didn't want today to be one of the days where she stayed in her car trying to calm herself down.

The report cards were being passed out and Caroline tried to use the breathing exercises that Dr. B always told her about. She wanted it to work. Desperately. Inhale

One. Two. Three. Four.

Exhale.

One. Two. Three. Four.

She was okay. She would be okay. And for the first time in a long time, she could feel her nerves leaving her and the panic subsiding. She *would* be okay.

Caroline was holding her report card in her hand without ever remembering when it got handed to her.

"All A's?" Izzy asked as she looked down at Caroline's report card.

Caroline looked down at her report card and saw only A's for her whole senior year. Ironically, school was the only thing she actually seemed to be able to focus on. "Yeah," she said absentmindedly.

Izzy gave her a questioning look and Caroline could not for the life of her figure out why Izzy was acting so weird.

"You're telling me that FSU didn't accept a straight A student?" Izzy blurted.

Caroline blinked slowly and turned to face Izzy. "Yeah," she said, trying so hard to sound convincing. "Why would you bring this up again, Iz? It sucks enough as it is." Caroline added that last part for emphasis and it seemed to make Izzy quiet but left Caroline feeling flushed and angry. She didn't really say another word to Izzy as she went to her next class, and then the next, and then the next as she tried to get through the day.

When it was time to leave, Caroline drove to Dr. B's for therapy. She still felt the anger inside her from Izzy questioning her—even if Izzy happened to be right. The only positive thing she could think of about the anger was the fact that it entirely got rid of her nerves. She couldn't think about anything else except for how mad she was.

As soon as she walked into Dr. B's office, she began pacing. She didn't even care that the bright yellow walls were mocking her. She didn't even think about the fact that Dr. B might tell her grandparents about her anger. She just had to get it out.

"Izzy had no right to be questioning me about FSU," Caroline said.

God bless Dr. B because she didn't even miss a beat. "Maybe she is worried you're making the wrong decision?" She was sitting at her desk watching as Caroline paced back and forth.

"It's not my decision to make if I didn't get in!" Caroline fumed. "I mean, she seriously thought that I was lying about getting rejected by FSU?" It felt so good to *feel* something. To be allowed to feel something without someone overanalyzing her emotions. She grumbled in frustration as she threw up her arms. "I mean, really," she laughed because it felt so good.

Dr. B paused. "Are you lying?"

Caroline stopped then. She looked over at Dr. B and wondered how she had let herself get so out of hand in front of her therapist. "No," she said flatly. "I'm not lying."

"Does it feel good to be angry?" Dr. B asked.

Caroline slumped down into one of the comfy chairs that was her usual home during those sessions. She felt defeated. Deflated. Damaged. "It feels better than anything else I've been feeling since Mom...." She stopped. The lump appeared in her throat faster than it ever had and she felt as if she was being choked.

"What else makes you angry?"

Caroline thought about this. Though the anger had left her, she tried to make it come back. "I'm mad that you think I need to be fixed."

Dr. B nodded.

"I'm angry that Grams thinks I need *pills* to be fixed." Caroline stood again, feeling the force of her anger as it came back. "I'm mad that I can't go to FSU. I'm mad that Izzy is questioning me. I'm mad that I can't seem to leave this place. *I'm so damn* angry that my mom died." Caroline felt the tears pricking her eyes. "And I'm so scared," she choked out.

The tears began falling down her cheeks.

"What are you scared of, Caroline?" Dr. B asked gently as she came up next to Caroline, gently placing her hand on Caroline's arm.

"I'm scared that I *can't* be fixed," she said softly as she swiped angrily at the tears cascading down her cheeks.

"Do you really want to be fixed?"

Caroline looked up at her therapist and took a step away from her. "Excuse me?" she said as she shook her head. "Don't you think I want to go back to normal? Don't you think I want to be able to go outside—to go on a freaking date—without worrying about whether or not I'll break? Whether or not I'll be able to breathe?"

"You've been coming to me for almost seven months, Caroline. This is the first time that you've opened up to me."

Caroline stared at the woman for a few moments, fully taking in what Dr. B was saying to her. "I've got to go," Caroline said as she wiped away the rest of her tears and grabbed her bag to leave.

***

<u>How to be normal on a double date:</u>
1. Wear something cute.
2. Keep the conversation on acceptable topics.
3. Definitely DON'T bring up college.
4. Be nice to Izzy.
5. Make sure to introduce Bennett to everyone.
6. Forget about Dr. B.

It didn't matter how many lists Caroline made, she couldn't seem to get the tingling sensation to leave her fingertips. She even shook her hands out as she waited for Bennett to get to her grandparents' house. She was going to ride with him to the bowling alley where they were meeting up with Izzy and Nick.

It was easy to accomplish the number one on her list. She was wearing jeans with lace-up boots and a cute sweater. Her hair was braided down her back and she felt like she could feign confidence looking at least a little confident in her outfit.

"Bennett's here Caroline!" she heard her Grams call.

Caroline took a deep breath as she closed her eyes. Once she opened them, she quickly grabbed her bag and headed to the front door.

Bennett had a bouquet of daisies for her and Caroline smiled. Grams was beaming and seemed more excited than Caroline did. "These are for you," he said as he smiled at her, pushing his glasses back up the bridge of his nose.

Caroline reached to grab the bouquet from him and quickly tip-toed up to kiss his cheek. He laughed nervously as she walked into the kitchen to find a vase. She put the flowers in them, feeling their delicate petals with her fingertips, and added a little water.

"I'm so glad Caroline is going out with you," Grams was saying when Caroline walked back to the front door. "She smiles so much when you're around."

"We're gonna go now, Grams," Caroline said as she walked up beside her grandmother. She kissed her cheek and took Bennett's hand as she led him out the house.

When they were outside, she looked over to Bennett and he looked just about as nervous as she felt. "You ready for this?" she asked.

"Is anyone ever really ready for a double date?" he asked sheepishly.

"No," Caroline laughed. "Definitely not."

They got in his car and drove to the bowling alley as Caroline gave Bennett a crash course on all things Izzy and Nick. Their relationship was everything Caroline imagined for Izzy. Together, Izzy and Nick were reckless. They were energetic and fervent and a whirlwind to be around. Caroline was never really sure if their relationship would last forever or if it would go up in flames. She, of course, hoped for the first option. Even if she was still mad at Izzy.

When they walked into the bowling alley and the introductions were out of the way, Caroline could tell that the night wouldn't be easy. Izzy had barely said a word to Caroline and that in itself signaled trouble.

As Bennett went to throw his ball down the alley, Nick started talking to Caroline. "So you're going to the pharmacy tech program?" He was being nice and trying to break the tension in the air and Caroline smiled at him for it. She appreciated the effort.

"Who even knows honestly," Izzy said as she came up behind them with her bowling ball.

Caroline looked up at her confusedly. Caroline knew that Izzy was angry, she just didn't realize it was to that extent.

"I mean," Caroline started, "I've applied to other colleges, but I just haven't gotten in anywhere that I'd want to go."

Bennett came up next to Caroline and both he and Nick were looking between her and Izzy. "You're lying," Izzy said as she very aggressively threw her ball down the alley, which resulted in a gutter ball.

"Excuse me?" Caroline said. Tingles started pricking the tips of her fingers again and it felt as if a hand was wrapping around her throat.

"You're lying," she repeated as she came back to the group and stared into Caroline's eyes.

"Oops, it's my turn," Nick said as he hopped up to go throw his bowling ball. Each of his moves looked exaggerated and almost as if he was in slow motion.

"I'm not lying, Izzy," Caroline choked out.

"Oh yeah?" Izzy challenged. "Then why do you have *six* acceptance letters in your drawer at your grandparents'?"

Caroline's heart dropped out of her chest. The world started spinning and she thought she would pass out if she didn't leave soon. Bennett subtly grabbed her hand, and it somehow grounded Caroline a little more.

"You went through my stuff?"

"You've been lying to everyone, Caroline. With the weird thing with the mail, you shoving it in that drawer, and let's not mention your report card. I mean, I *knew* something was up. I just don't understand why you have to lie about it!" Izzy was shouting now and it looked like there were tears in her eyes.

Caroline wasn't sure how much more she could take. She stood up shakily from her seat and grabbed her bag. She tugged at Bennett's hand to let him know what she was doing. "We're leaving."

"Caroline," Izzy said as she grabbed her arm. "I just don't understand. We're *best* friends. I just—I thought you'd tell me what was wrong."

Caroline shrugged her off and just walked away. She was at the very dangerous edge of a cliff that would have her falling into the darkness. It felt as if she would fall so far that she'd never find her way back up.

Bennett came up behind her and touched her shoulder. She flinched and tried to hold back the tears.

"Caroline, what happened back there?"

"I-I—Bennett—" Caroline tried to speak, but her voice was quaking. "Just t-take me home, p-please." She blinked and a tear fell down her cheek as they walked to his car. She was about to break again. She wasn't sure if she could take it again so soon. She shivered and took in a shaky breath as Bennett began to drive.

Chapter 10

Somehow, Caroline was able to compose herself on the drive back to her grandparents'. Bennett had offered his hand to her and she had grabbed it gratefully. The whole drive, he had rubbed smooth circles on the back of her hand.

When they pulled up to her grandparents' house, she could see that her Gramps' car was gone, but the lights in the house were still on. She assumed that he left to go check something out at the pharmacy since Caroline hadn't worked that day.

"Are you okay?" Bennett asked. The look of concern on his face made Caroline's chest hurt. She didn't want to make other people worried. She didn't want to be broken. She wanted to be whole, but it felt as if so many tiny pieces of her were missing.

"I'm fine," she croaked, and then tried to clear her throat. "I'll be fine."

"Do you want to talk about it?" he asked.

She shook her head almost violently.

He leaned in close to her and hesitantly held her cheek with one hand. It was comforting in a way that Caroline couldn't describe, but she leaned on his hand and tried to take as much of this feeling as she could get.

"I told you I wasn't good at dates," he said quietly with a small smile inching up his cheeks.

Caroline laughed. "That definitely had nothing to do with you, but I appreciate you for being so great during that disaster." She took her face away from his hand and it suddenly felt very cold. "Maybe next time it could just be you and me?"

"I'd like that," Bennett smiled.

So, Caroline said goodbye and got out of his car. She walked up the driveway and turned around to wave at him. He waited until she was inside to drive off. It made her feel even more at ease.

When Caroline got inside, though, her body went cold. "Grams?" she called throughout the house. "Gramps?"

No one answered her.

She called her Grams on her cell phone.

"We just went out on a date. Are you home already?"

No. "No, no," Caroline could hear her voice saying. "I just wanted to check up on you guys." She sounded normal. So normal. But she was choking.

Breathe.

"Okay, sweetie, call us if you need us. We should be home in about two hours."

Two hours? She hung up the phone. Inhale.

One. Two. Three. Four.

Everything was getting dark. The house was so small. So empty. *You're alone.* Her fingers began to feel numb and her chest hurt so much. *Breathe.*

She began pacing in the living room, trying to calm herself down. Caroline pulled out her phone, but her hands were shaking so much that she dropped it.

You're going to die.

A sob ripped through her throat as she fell to her knees to grab her phone. She curled in on herself. She couldn't breathe. She was choking. *Breathe. You're lying. It's what she would've wanted.*

You're alone.

She screamed angrily at the top of her lungs as she beat the ground and began to hyperventilate. She was going to die alone.

Caroline grasped at her phone and somehow was able to open it and dial his number.

"Caroline?" Bennett said through the phone.

"I-I—" Caroline tried to get out, but she was choking. She was dying.

"Are you okay? Caroline?"

"Please come," she cried. "P-please."

"I'm turning around. I'll be there in a few minutes. Stay on the phone with me," he sounded panicked.

She tried to breathe. She tried to get in a breath but her damn lungs wouldn't work. She gasped.

"Tell me about yearbook," she heard Bennett say over the phone. "Tell me about your favorite picture that you've taken so far."

Inhale.

One. Two. Three. Four.

"It's o-of you," she breathed out.

He was quiet for a moment. "The one at the track meet?"

She nodded but then said, "Yeah." Her hands were shaking so badly that she was afraid she'd drop the phone. Then she'd lose Bennett. *You're alone.*

Caroline shook her head as another sob escaped her throat.

"I'm coming, Caroline. I'm almost there."

"Hurry," she wanted to say. She couldn't get the word to leave her lips, though.

It wasn't long before Bennett came through the door that Caroline had left unlocked. He found her on her knees in the living room and rushed over to her. He knelt down beside her. She was hugging herself so tightly that he nearly had to pry her hands off herself. Caroline was shaking violently as he wrapped his arms tightly around her. Bennett held her, almost having her in his lap from how close they were.

"I-I'm s-sorry," Caroline cried. "I-I'm b-broken."

He played in her hair, shushing her, soothing her as she cried.

Breathe.

Breathe.

She could breathe.

"I'm here," he soothed. "I'm here for you, Caro."

He was there. She could breathe. And so she did.

One. Two. Three. Four.

He held her as she calmed down and they fell into complete silence except for the shushing noises Bennett made as he stroked her face. She held onto his arm tightly, half on his lap and half off, her legs tucked beneath her. She felt empty, drained, completely devoid of life and she didn't know what to say to Bennett now that he witnessed her breaking.

Caroline looked out across the living room, trying to latch on to a single thought, but all of her thoughts were gone. Everything was gone.

"You could've told me about this," Bennett said softly as he twirled a lock of her hair around his finger.

"I could've told a lot of people," she said—her voice flat and monotonal—thinking of Izzy.

"What—" Bennett started. "What exactly is it?"

Caroline stared at the floor, and she knew he couldn't see her face, but she still felt the flush of embarrassment hit her. "It's nothing."

"My brother was depressed," he started. "And not in the way that you use the word just to describe someone who has had a bad day. He couldn't shake it. It was with him all the time and he couldn't make it go away." Bennett held her hand tightly, rubbing each of her fingers down to her fingertips. "And the only reason—the only reason I knew about it was because he told me. And I'm sure you know all about this because everyone in this town talks, but it was just—it was really hard to see him go through that. He made me promise not to talk to our parents about it. I think that promise is what killed him."

Caroline sighed then, knowing that she had to tell him something. Knowing that she couldn't let him sit there and worry if she would do the same thing that his brother did. "It's not like that for me, Bennett. I swear. It's more of like me thinking that I'll die, not wanting to, and freaking out about it." Caroline paused, still not wanting to give him more information than that. She didn't want to name it. If she gave it a name, it became real. It defined her. It became the reason for her brokenness. If she could just hide its name, she could hide the rest the same way she's been doing for those past few months. "I see a therapist for it."

"Did she tell you what it—"

"Yes," Caroline interrupted. "And I don't wanna talk about it."

Bennett nodded. She rested her cheek on his abdomen.

"Remember how I told you I can't be alone? How it started when my mom died? No one else knows about it. Just you and me." Caroline picked at a hangnail as she continued. "I've tried so hard to keep it from everyone else. My grandparents have seen me freak out before, but they don't know why. They don't know that it happens every time I'm alone, and I've tried so hard to be normal and whole and an actual person that I just—"

"Caroline," Bennett stopped her as he picked her up to a sitting position so she could meet his eyes. "These feelings? Whatever they told you this is? It doesn't make you any less of a person."

"Yes, it does," she said fiercely. "I can't do normal things. I can't go out on my own and be alone and be anywhere where people aren't. It makes me so broken that sometimes I wonder if I'll ever be fixed."

"My brother committed suicide because he thought his depression defined him. He thought that all he could ever be was a diagnosis. He didn't get help but you have the chance to let people help you. Izzy just wants to help you. *I* want to help you, Caroline."

Caroline stared at him, at his warm brown eyes and coffee skin. She saw his kindness and his pain and his vulnerability. "Then just help me forget," she said as she reached over, softly grabbing his face, and kissed him.

It was a soft kiss. One that wasn't rushed and wasn't impassioned, but rather, it was sad and sweet and all the emotions that they had both felt in their lives. It was both new to Caroline and not. A swirl of emotions that she couldn't pin down or define.

"I don't want to help you forget," Bennett whispered when they pulled away, their foreheads resting against one another's.

Caroline couldn't say anything. What was there to say? "I'll be fine, Bennett," she said because it was the only thing she could say.

"A lie that is half-truth is the darkest of all lies," Bennett murmured.

"Tennyson," Caroline said, recognizing the part of the poem.

Bennett nodded and Caroline wondered what they were teaching him in preparation for law school. She wondered how he even wanted to be a lawyer. It didn't seem like him.

Caroline's phone buzzed and it was her Gramps texting to say that they were on their way home and that they'd be there in ten minutes.

"You should go," Caroline said to Bennett. "It's getting late and my grandparents are almost back."

He nodded at her as he stood up and helped her to her feet. "You'll be okay?" he asked gently.

She nodded back at him. "I'll be okay."

With her answer, he turned towards the door to leave.

"Bennett!" she called, walking up beside him. She put her hand on his cheek, holding him the same way he held her on the way home. "Thank you." Caroline tip-toed up to kiss him quickly on his lips.

Bennett smiled sadly and nodded one last time, leaving without saying another word.

Chapter 11

The next morning, Caroline woke up late for a Saturday. She had missed breakfast, she was sure of it, but was more surprised that her Grams hadn't called her down.

After Bennett had left last night, Caroline waited only for five minutes before her grandparents got home. Granted, even though she was emotionally exhausted, it still felt like the longest five minutes of her life, but her grandparents still didn't know that anything was wrong. That's how Caroline wanted to keep it.

They had gone to bed shortly after that and Caroline went up to her room. Like so many nights before, she stared up at the ceiling. She thought about Izzy. She thought about Bennett and how her first kiss with him was fueled by emotions she didn't want. But most of all, though, she thought about her mom. She thought about the night she died. Caroline thought about her mother asking her to stay home—to spend time with her—but Caroline saying that she had plans she couldn't cancel.

It hurt to think about all the things that had happened in those past seven months. It hurt so much that Caroline often felt like puking. She thought about her mother and everything that she went through. Still, her mother overcame everything. Why couldn't Caroline do that? Why couldn't she fix herself?

It was sometime in between those thoughts that she had finally fallen asleep, but it had already been late enough for her to see the sun peeking through her windows. Which is why Caroline wasn't surprised in the first place that she had woken up so late.

When she checked her phone, it was nearly eleven in the morning. Bennett had sent her a text about two hours ago. It made her smile in a way that let her forget her thoughts.

SAT – 9:08 AM
Bennett: Can I see you today?

SAT – 11:19 AM
Caroline: I'd love that.

SAT – 11:21 AM
Bennett: Lunch? I'll come pick you up.

SAT – 11:22 AM
Caroline: That sounds perfect.

Caroline got out of bed and began getting ready. She put a little makeup on and braided her hair in one long braid down her back. She threw on some clothes, and then went to leave.

She couldn't find her Grams or Gramps, but after walking around the house for a moment, she heard them talking outside in the back. Instead of interrupting them, she decided to leave a note just as Bennett's text came through letting her know that he was waiting for her outside.

When Caroline got into Bennett's car, he looked uncertain and shy and everything that seemed to make up Bennett Williams. She smiled brightly at him to take that look away. It worked and he smiled back at her, his eyes crinkling at the corners.

"You look… good," he started, sounding very unsure of himself.

Caroline chose to bring humor into the conversation instead of dwelling on what happened last night. "I know," she started, striking a pose, "I put a lot of work into this outfit." Considering that her outfit was more along the lines of hobo than cute, she laughed.

He started driving and Caroline wasn't sure where he was taking her. A few minutes passed before he spoke again.

"I told you, I don't want to help you forget," he said softly.

Caroline looked down at her fingers and began methodically clenching and unfurling them. She didn't know what to say to him. How was she supposed to open up to him when she couldn't even say what was wrong with her out loud? How was she supposed to let him in when he still didn't know about the pills she never took hiding in her cabinet, her dreams about FSU and using him to distract her from the decision deadline coming up in two months, or even about her mother and how badly Caroline had let her down? There were still so many things that she was keeping hidden, and with what happened to his brother? Would he judge her more or less?

"Bennett," she started slowly, still looking down at her fingers. The prickling feeling began crawling up her neck. The lump appeared in her throat as if it had never left. "I'm trying—" she cleared her throat. "I'm trying to let you in. I'm trying to tell you things that I can't tell anyone else. It's just—it's gonna take me some time." She inhaled.

One. Two. Three. Four.

She exhaled, inhaled, exhaled, and all of her tension went away. She could breathe without a problem. She stopped fidgeting with her fingers. Maybe she would be okay.

He reached out to hold her hand and she let him. "I know," he said, "and I can wait. I just don't want to be the person who lets you forget."

Caroline intertwined her fingers in his and she felt as if there was more pain in those words than he was letting on, but she wasn't going to press him on it. There were some things that had to surface by themselves. She just hoped that they both could reach the surface instead of sinking.

"So, where exactly are you taking me?" Caroline asked, a smile teasing the corners of her lips.

Bennett looked over at her and smiled. "It's a surprise."

***

"So," Bennett started as Caroline grimaced. "I know we both agreed that hiking wasn't our idea of fun…."

Caroline looked up at the trail in front of her. It was an actual marked trailhead, so that made Caroline feel better, but she absolutely hated being that far from help. After picking up a quick lunch, they had driven up winding roads to get there. Caroline could see canyons and mountains all around her. They were currently in a national park, although she couldn't remember for the life of her the name of it.

"Bennett—"

"It's not far, I promise," he said with a small smile on his lips. He looked apologetic and Caroline really didn't want to protest. It was, after all, a surprise.

She looked at her phone and saw one bar of service. It made her nervous to think that they wouldn't have a way to call for help if the service went out, but he promised her it wasn't far. The cell service couldn't go out that easily, right?

When Caroline finally reluctantly agreed, Bennett pulled a backpack from his car and Caroline knew he had been planning this. She eyed him suspiciously and he shrugged, a shy smile framing his face.

Together, they began to hike up the incline, but it wasn't too bad. If Caroline had to be honest, it was very scenic and wasn't strenuous. She could see trees and canyons and even a river. It wasn't even thirty minutes before Bennett stopped. He took her hand and looked at her, asking her to trust him. She nodded because she wasn't sure what else to do. That was when he started leading her off-trail. Though, Caroline could tell that the path they were taking had been walked a few times, and it didn't take them long before Bennett stopped again.

They had made it to a small cliffside that looked out at the canyon below them. It was beautiful and made Caroline shiver. Bennett came up behind her and slipped something around her arms. It was the jacket-blanket, and Caroline couldn't help laughing. She turned to face him, but noticed something behind him. She squinted at it and something pinched in her chest as she realized what it said.

Josh was here.

"I don't know when he did this," Bennett said quietly. They both stared at the weathered plank of wood, the words carved deep into it. It looked as if someone—presumably Josh—had brought it there and wedged it in a place that it would never leave.

It hurt Caroline to look at the words. She could feel Josh's pain writing that because she understood, in a way, how it felt. Even if she didn't experience the same pain as he did, she knew what it felt like to wonder if you were going to disappear. Caroline was afraid of dying. Josh had wanted just that.

"I come up here a lot to remind myself that in certain places, he is still here. He hasn't disappeared completely. I've never shown my dad this place, or my mom. Their way of healing was to act like it never happened. They never let themselves hurt. I think, though, that the reason they don't want to feel is because they've never forgiven themselves."

"I wish I would've known him better," Caroline said quietly, still staring at the letters carved into the wood.

"Me too."

She reached out for his hand and held it tightly. Maybe he needed someone to lean on just as much as she did. It made her feel bad to think of how heavily she'd been relying on him to help her forget her problems.

"The reason I brought you here, Caroline, is that I wanted to remind you that *you* are still here," Bennett said as he turned her around to face the canyons. "I know you want to forget. I know you feel scared and trapped and broken." He held her hand as they walked closer to the edge. Then, he sat down and she sat down next to him. They were facing the trees, the edge, the canyons, the river. They were facing everything. "But you *are* still here, and so am I."

He made her feel alive in ways that she couldn't ever remember feeling since her mother died. He made her want to fight and to face her fears and go to FSU. As she looked out at the vast expanse of nothingness, though, she knew that he alone would never be enough. He couldn't fix her no matter how much she wanted him to. Because even with him there, that vast expanse still scared her. She could still feel her fingers tingling and her hands shaking as she thought about being out of cell range if something bad happened.

Bennett wanted her to heal. Bennett wanted her to be okay. He wanted her to be there. How was she supposed to do that? How was she supposed to convince her own mind that she was fine?

In the end, they sat there for a long time. Caroline ended up sitting between Bennett's outstretched legs as he wrapped his arms around her. She hadn't wanted to get up, but the waning sun forced them both to leave.

When they got back to the car, Caroline's phone went berserk with notifications. She had several texts from her Grams telling her to come home as well as at least three missed calls. Bile began rising up in Caroline's stomach because there was no explanation for why her Grams seemed so frantic.

"Can you take me home?" Caroline said, her voice sounding shaky.

"Is something wrong?" he asked.

She looked at him, having the familiar feeling of fingers wrapping around her throat and squeezing. Caroline practiced her breathing techniques, and then said, "I don't know." Then she threw her stuff in his car and got in the passenger seat, sitting on her hands to keep them from shaking.

Chapter 12

When they got back to Caroline's grandparents' house and Caroline saw Izzy's car in the driveway, she nearly puked. Something was very *very* wrong and she was terrified to find out what it was. The last time she felt like that was the moment she unlocked the door to her house and it was silent. Her mother was silent.

You're alone.

She wanted to start crying, but she knew she was overreacting. Maybe it was nothing. Maybe it was something simple like Grams asking her what she wanted for dinner. She should've just called Grams back, but she couldn't risk shutting down again in front of Bennett.

"I can come in with you?" he asked, lightly touching her shoulder.

She shook her head, but then sucked in a ragged breath.

Breathe.

Caroline got out without another word and grabbed her things. The walk up the driveway felt like it took forever. When she got to the front door and pushed it open, the atmosphere around her changed. She stepped inside and saw her Gramps sitting at a chair in the dining room. She saw Grams pacing beside him. She saw Izzy sitting next to Gramps at the table. They were all okay. They were fine.

"What's going on?" she asked.

Izzy, Grams, and Gramps looked over to her. Gramps looked sad. Izzy looked guilty. Grams looked… *pissed*.

"You tell me, Caroline," Grams said as she shook several sheets of paper in her hand.

Caroline looked back at Izzy and Izzy looked at the floor. "You showed her my letters?" Caroline asked, absolutely stunned. It was one thing that Izzy called her out on it. It was a completely different realm of horrible that she showed them to her grandparents.

"They told me about what's been going on," Izzy said. "You're holding yourself back. Caro, I had to."

"No, you didn't!" Caroline nearly shrieked.

"This isn't Isabelle's fault," Grams said, slapping each individual letter down on the dining room table. "I know you've been having a tough time since Elizabeth died, but—"

"Mom has nothing to do with this," Caroline said, feeling her emotions getting wildly out of control.

"Then what about the pills, Caroline?" Grams said, her voice raising an octave. "I mean, we have never been the type of people to invade your privacy, but you make me feel like we should have been!"

The world started spinning around her. The edges of her vision turned black. She vaguely registered the smell of vegetable soup on the stove. "They…" Caroline tried to say. "They…."

"They're supposed to help you, but they can't do anything if you just keep stacking them in your cabinet!" Grams said as her arms flew down to her sides. She was gesturing crazily as she spoke to Caroline. "What happened to your mother was just a—"

"A freak accident!" Caroline shouted, tears spilling down the corners of her eyes. "*I know that.*"

"Then why won't you take them? We know that they're safe for you. We wouldn't give you something that would hurt you. Don't you know that?" Grams sighed and put her hand up to her eyes, rubbing her temples.

"I don't want them," Caroline choked out.

"Just like you *swear* you don't want to go to FSU?"

"Yes," Caroline squeaked.

"Then why lie about getting accepted to all of these colleges, Caroline? Why would you lie about that?"

"I don't know," she mumbled.

"You do know. You just won't tell us," Grams said heavily, taking a seat at the dining room table. "I'm signing you up for a tour at FSU. You have to go. You have to start taking your medication. You *have* to stop lying."

Caroline's heart dropped. She couldn't go on a tour of FSU. It would make it hurt so much more when she couldn't go. She definitely couldn't take her meds….

You're going to die.

Caroline stared down at the floor. Izzy knew about the colleges. She knew about Caroline's brokenness. They all knew about the medicine.

"Caroline?"

She turned around to see Bennett in the hallway behind her. Now he knew about everything, too.

Caroline turned back to face Izzy. "How could you?" she said, the tears choking her words. She pushed past Bennett back into the hallway, grabbing the keys to her car, and rushing outside to get in. She drove off before anyone could stop her.

Breathe.

Fix it.

You're going to die.

She drove as far as she could. It was completely dark outside, and her headlights barely illuminated anything once she got outside of town.

Caroline couldn't go on a tour at FSU. She couldn't enroll there. She couldn't live in Florida all by herself.

You're alone.

It's what she would've wanted.

It was so *damn* loud in her head. She couldn't make herself stop. She couldn't stop the darkness, and once she realized how far outside of town she was, the darkness didn't even have to try.

You're alonealonealonealone.

Even if she could stop thinking, she was so far gone that she wasn't sure if she would've wanted to stop. She wanted to hurt and the feeling was so toxic that it overtook her entire body. She screamed and pulled over to the side of the road as she began beating on her steering wheel.

You're alone.

She began to hyperventilate. She couldn't be alone. She couldn't go to FSU. She couldn't do it.

Fix it.

She locked her car and crawled into the backseat, rocking herself as she cried and tried to breathe.

You're going to die.

She looked out the back windshield and saw the sign.

Welcome to Valor City, Arizona!

Caroline was only feet away from the city limits when she had started to break. That was the furthest she could go by herself.

You're alone.

Breathe.

It's what she would've wanted.

As her chest felt like it was going to explode, her lungs ached from lack of air, and her tears flew down her cheeks, she knew she couldn't be alone. She knew she couldn't go to FSU. She had just proven it to herself.

***

"Thank you for meeting me," Caroline said softly. The yellow walls surrounding her mocked her for being there. She didn't belong in that brightly painted room, but she needed to talk.

"I'm glad you called me, Caroline," Dr. B said. "I'm sorry it took me so long to get here."

Caroline shook her head. By the time she had called Dr. B, she was so drained that she didn't have it in her to feel the fear that she felt before. She felt stoic and subdued and empty and so *so* tired.

She had just filled Dr. B in on everything that had transpired that evening with her grandparents, Izzy, and Bennett. It felt like too much to carry, but it felt a little better when she said it out loud.

"Why did you lie to them about your acceptance at FSU?" Dr. B asked.

"I'm surprised you didn't want to ask me about the medicine first," Caroline said with a humorless smile.

The older woman shook her head, seeming not concerned about it. "The medication isn't what worries me. What worries me is what is causing you to have these panic attacks so often."

Panic attacks. Words Caroline had avoided so well.

She looked down at her feet. She thought for a long time about what to say. She'd never been this open with her therapist, but, God, did she want someone to know the full truth instead of picking up the pieces she left behind.

When Caroline didn't answer, Dr. B said, "Why did you call me here tonight?" It was a gentle question, but Caroline knew its purpose.

"To talk," she murmured.

Dr. B nodded encouragingly at Caroline.

"I can't—I can't—" she tried. She had already told Bennett this. It shouldn't be hard to tell Dr. B, too. "I can't be alone."

A nod of recognition came from Dr. B. It was as if a lightbulb had gone off over her therapist's head. "And you can't go to FSU without having to be alone."

Despite Caroline's exhaustion, tears flooded her eyes again. She couldn't stop them. She sobbed uncontrollably as Dr. B brought a box of tissues and sat down next to her, putting her arm around Caroline.

"You know what I think?" Dr. B asked.

Caroline stopped crying for a moment to look up at her.

"I think you should go tour FSU—"

"Oh," Caroline groaned, throwing her hands up in exasperation, "not you too."

Dr. B laughed and Caroline felt a small smile teasing at the edges of her lips. "Take someone with you. Someone you trust and feel comfortable around. I know you're mad at Isabelle and your grandparents, but any of them would love to go with you."

Caroline shook her head, knowing that she couldn't take them. It would be awkward after all that had happened. Maybe Bennett, though….

"Once you get back," Dr. B started, "we can talk again."

"And the meds?" Caroline asked reluctantly.

"I can't force you to take them, Caroline. Even if I think they'll help you. But I think I understand why you don't want to."

Caroline looked at her therapist and wondered how someone could become so receptive as a person. She guessed that's why she was a therapist.

"You really think they'd make it stop?" Caroline asked, feeling vulnerable and exposed.

"Maybe not completely, but it would make a huge difference."

Caroline smiled at the woman and felt a little lighter after ranting about her grandparents and talking about her fears. "Then maybe we can talk about those next time, too."

Dr. B's smile put the yellow walls to shame.

Caroline took a deep breath and patted both of her knees as she stood up. She let out a huff of air, "Okay," she started. "I think it's time for me to go. It's getting late."

"Looks like I need to look into late night therapy sessions," Dr. B joked. "They seem to work a lot better."

Caroline shook her head, "I think it had more to do with you."

Dr. B looked down, but shook her head as well. "This journey—everything that happens along the way—has *everything* to do with you. You made the choice to call."

Chapter 13

Caroline was absentmindedly going over the warning labels on all of the different medications as she attached them to each packaged prescription. It was Monday and she had hardly spoken to anyone since Saturday when everything had gone to shit.

She wasn't quite sure what to do now. Things were so irreparably broken and all of her plans were botched, so where did that leave her? She couldn't face her grandparents. She couldn't face Izzy. She couldn't even face Bennett after he had presumably witnessed her all-consuming humiliation served to her on a silver platter by her Grams.

The problem was that no one understood. No one fully grasped what she was going through. She didn't think Dr. B understood, but at least she listened. No one else listened. No one else *heard* her.

Caroline didn't want to go to FSU—well *couldn't* go to FSU. She was okay with going to the community college. It was a good education. It would save money for her grandparents. She would never have to leave Arizona. But that, in itself, was convoluted. She wouldn't have to leave Arizona, but she would *never* leave Arizona.

She let out a huge sigh as she sunk her head into her hands.

"You sound very…"

Caroline turned to look at the person speaking to her.

"…pensive," Curtis finished. "Does it have anything to do with the fact that your grandfather is now avoiding the pharmacy when you're here."

Caroline shrugged. "I think he's scared of me."

Curtis laughed deeply. "What happened?"

"It doesn't matter," Caroline said, waving him off.

"Looks like it matters a lot," he said quietly.

She took a deep breath in and everything—all of her problems—just started spewing out of her mouth. "So all this time I've been hiding my college acceptances because I didn't want anyone to know about them. Well, my so-called best friend snooped in my stuff, found all the letters, and *showed* them to my grandparents. Now everyone thinks I actually want to go to FSU and Grams is making me tour the campus and I just—"

Curtis held up a hand. "You *do* want to go there, though. You always talked about it. Not just a few times a year. Always. Since you were a freshman."

"That's not the point, Curtis," she said with a lot more attitude than she intended to have.

"This reminds me a lot of a cinematic masterpiece of a movie," he started.

"You think all movies are cinematic masterpieces," she said as she rolled her eyes.

"That's not the point, *Caroline*," he said, mirroring her earlier sass. "It was about a boy who held back on everything. He skipped out on things that scared him or that he thought was unimportant. He ended up halfway through his twenties before he had even realized what he'd done."

"What happened?"

"He stayed inside. He lived through movies, watching each one and knowing that they were all special. They all had a story to tell, which made all of them worth watching."

"Curtis…" Caroline started slowly. "Are you talking about yourself?"

Curtis smiled in a weird sensei-teaching-you-a-lesson kind of way and Caroline cocked her head at him. He was so strange sometimes, but it was his weirdness that Caroline loved him for. He had been working at the pharmacy since he was nineteen and she wasn't even in high school yet. Occasionally, she would get that sensei look from him. He would always use movies as an analogy. Never his own life. Which kind of made Caroline sad in a way. Especially since he just basically alluded to the rest of her life if she kept this up.

"My point is that you need to get out there. You can't let *you* hold you back. Go to FSU." Curtis shrugged his shoulders and stuck his hands in his pockets. "Take it from someone who's already seen this movie."

"So, are you saying that your life is a cinematic masterpiece?" Caroline giggled to lighten the mood a little bit.

"No," Curtis said as he shook his head with a smile, "but it could be, and isn't that the point of it all?"

As he went back to the front to let her sit and think about what he said, Caroline really wondered if the point was the potential. They each started out with blank slates. Nothing and no one to write the story for them. They could either be the main characters, or someone without recognition during the credits. It was the potential that drove them forward. The idea that there could be greatness if they could just overcome their own obstacles.

But the question that Caroline always landed on was how? How do you overcome a problem that you couldn't even see? She wished it were something tangible. Something visible. Like a tumor. At least then there was something to blame her emotions and feelings and fear on.

She knew better, though. Nothing was better or worse or easier. It was all just a different kind of darkness from her own.

When her eyes landed on a warning label that brought a pang to her chest, she began to think of how all of it had started. Her happiness had died with her mother. With choking and silent screams and a throat closing and a face turning blue. It all started with one tiny little pill.

Allergy alert: may cause a severe allergic reaction. If an allergic reaction occurs, stop use and seek medical help right away.

Her mother never had the chance to seek help. Caroline couldn't think about it, though, because she would be pulled so far under that she wouldn't be able to function for the rest of the day. She had to be able to function in order to convince Bennett to go with her to Florida. That was if he didn't think she was completely mental now. But she *had* to convince him. She didn't think she could survive that trip with anyone else at the moment.

There was a light knock on the door behind her. She honestly didn't know anyone who would knock on that door instead of just walking in.

"Caro?"

It was Izzy and Caroline's stomach roiled at the sound of her voice. She stayed quiet as Izzy walked up behind her.

"I wanted to talk to you," Izzy started quietly.

Caroline hadn't turned around in her seat yet to face her. "I don't want to talk."

"Caro," Izzy said. Caroline felt Izzy's hand touch her shoulder.

She flinched away from Izzy's touch and turned to face her. "I said I don't want to talk to you."

Izzy's expression almost broke Caroline's heart. Despite the anger and the feeling of betrayal, seeing Izzy hurting the way that she obviously was made Caroline hurt.

Caroline closed her eyes and took a deep breath before opening them again. "You hurt me, Izzy."

Izzy looked down at her feet. "You hurt me, too, Caro."

Caroline wasn't sure what to say after that. She wanted to stay angry. She wanted to hate Izzy and be mean to her and say things that would hurt her. The thing was, though, Caroline was never like that. She didn't hold grudges. She could barely stay angry for more than a few hours let alone days.

"I don't know what to say to you," Caroline said.

"Can I say some things then?" Izzy asked, her doe eyes staring hopefully at Caroline.

She nodded.

"I just—" Izzy started. "I thought I had to tell them. I didn't understand what was going on. I didn't know all of this stuff that was going on with you and—"

Caroline almost tuned out for a bit. She was watching the way that Izzy was looking at her. Like she was broken. Damaged. Caroline wished she could take it all back. Every single thing that she did in front of Izzy to lead her to that stupid drawer with those stupid college letters. At least then, Izzy would have never found them, and she would have *never* found out about Caroline.

"—Izzy, just stop," Caroline said as she raised her hand up to quiet her. "Stop looking at me like you feel bad for me. Just... stop."

"I'm sorry, I just—" Izzy stuttered. "I just don't know what to do to make it better."

"You didn't have to tell my grandparents, you know."

"I thought... I just didn't understand... Caroline," Izzy said, exasperated, "FSU has been your *dream* for as long as I can remember. You never stopped talking about it. The fact that I found an acceptance letter from them and you kept telling everyone that you didn't get in made me so worried. It made me think you wanted to die or something, I mean, I don't know."

"I don't want to die," Caroline said calmly. "I've never wanted to die."

"I know that *now*. I just didn't know that *then*. You have to think about what that looked like to me.

I mean, Caro, you skip class a lot. You skipped it for a whole week a few weeks ago. I just—I don't want to lose you. I was so scared of losing you."

Caroline sighed. She guessed it did look really bad from Izzy's perspective. "Then why didn't you talk to me about it?"

"I tried—"

"No, you didn't," Caroline interrupted. "You basically started attacking me for not telling you about it. That's not talking to me."

Tears came to Izzy's eyes and Caroline felt a lump form in her own throat. She hated to see Izzy hurting but how was she supposed to fix it if Izzy was the one who had hurt her?

"You're right," Izzy sniffled. "I'm sorry. But, Caro, would you have really told me everything if I had asked?"

No. "Maybe."

Izzy looked back down to her shoes, tears falling from her eyes. "I just don't understand why you didn't tell me."

"Because you would've done exactly what you're doing now: look at me like I'm broken and force me to go to FSU."

"But you *want* to go to FSU, Caro."

"No, I don't," Caroline said forcefully, both telling her the truth and a lie at the same time. If only it was a simple yes or no answer. It was so much more complicated than that for Caroline. No one but Bennett—and Dr. B now—knew that Caroline was terrified of being alone. Florida was as alone as it could get for her.

Izzy was silent for a moment, staring at Caroline as if she was trying to figure her out. "Then why did you apply?" Izzy kept eye contact with Caroline, not backing down this time. She wasn't going to let it go and Caroline could tell. "If you really wanted to go to the community college, why apply to *all* of those other colleges? You want to leave Arizona, Caro, I know you do. You're scared of something. I don't know if it has something to do with your mom or something to do with your grandparents, but you're holding yourself back."

"I can't—" Caroline squeaked. She cleared her throat and tried to start again. "I can't go to FSU."

Izzy reached for Caroline's hand and squeezed it. "All I know, Caro, is that you've been dealing with this for so long by yourself. I don't know what it's like for you, but I know that you must've been scared each time. I know you were probably hurting. I also know that you are so strong for carrying this all by yourself, but do you know what my mom always says?"

Caroline reached up and wiped her eyes, not realizing until then that she had begun to cry. She shook her head and Izzy continued.

"She says that it makes you stronger when you decide to hold the burden with someone else because sometimes, it is harder to let others help carry your problems than it is to just carry them yourself." Izzy watched as Caroline cried and wrapped her arms around her.

Caroline cried silently into her friend's shoulder. "It's not your burden to carry."

Izzy pulled away from Caroline and wiped away her own tears. "Excuse me?" Izzy said defensively. "It's your problem so therefore it is *my* problem. That's how it's always been for us."

Caroline laughed a little through her tears.

"And that's even if you won't tell me what the problem is," Izzy said into Caroline's hair.

Caroline pulled away after a moment and wiped away the rest of her tears. "I can't..." she started. "I'm still mad at you."

Izzy nodded solemnly. "I know. You can still tell me what's wrong, though.... If you want."

Caroline shook her head quickly. She couldn't deal with it at the moment. She didn't even want to think about it. It was everything that caused her to have that intense fear of being alone. How it all had started. No one knew that part. Not even Bennett.

Nodding, Izzy finally let go of Caroline's hand. "I love you, Caro."

"I love you too, Iz."

"Maybe I'll see you later?"

Caroline nodded and tried to offer her a small smile. "Maybe."

Chapter 14

Caroline had just gotten off of work. It was past dinnertime, so it was hard to think of an excuse to get Bennett to meet her. She ended up sticking to coffee even though she knew she'd never sleep that night if she did get coffee.

"Coffee?" he had asked over the phone.

Caroline felt like it was safer to call him because at least then she could hear his voice and what he was feeling. The problem, though, was that she couldn't tell *anything*. He sounded so… monotonal. There was nothing to give Caroline an indication of how he was feeling or how he felt about her. It made her extremely nervous.

"Yes… coffee…." She had said slowly.

So, there she was, waiting in a booth with a cup of regular black coffee in front of her. She was doctoring it up with sugar and creamer and anything to get it to be a little less bitter. When it finally tasted consumable, she began writing on a napkin, trying to calm herself down.

Things to do with Bennett in Florida:

1. Tour campus : (
2. Go to the Sweet Shop (where Mom and Dad met).
3. Picnic at Landis Green.
4. Go to the beach (because we're in Florida and it's a must).
5. Feed the seagulls.
6. Don't think.

She finished her list and began stirring her coffee absentmindedly. She had probably stirred it five or six times by the time Bennett walked into the café.

Caroline breathed out a sigh of relief that he had at least shown up. She wasn't sure how he'd feel after the disaster he had witnessed Saturday.

"Bennett," she breathed.

"Caroline," he said, smiling in an odd, sad little way.

"I'm glad you came. I—" she started. "I have a lot to explain to you."

He nodded.

That was it.

A nod.

So, she cleared her throat uncomfortably and continued. "You must think that I'm crazy for—"

He held up his hand to stop her. Bennett sighed tiredly and Caroline felt the knots twisting in her stomach as a lump formed in her throat. This was it. He was going to tell her that he couldn't handle being around her.

"You don't get it, Caroline," he said. "I *don't* think you're crazy. Not a single bit. I do think it's not smart that you've been hiding your meds instead of taking them. What do you plan to do with all of them?"

She could hear the panic in his voice as he asked that question. She could see him connecting dots that weren't there. "Bennett, I don't want to die." Caroline reached over and held his hand from across the booth. "I *don't* want to die," she said more forcefully. "That's the whole reason I haven't been taking the pills."

"What do you mean?"

She felt everything inside of her tighten as she braced for the impact of her memories. Her own memories and experiences that had wreaked so much havoc on her life. Caroline had to tell him. It didn't matter that the gossip had spread like wildfire in her small town when her mother had died. It didn't matter because she and her grandparents had never told anyone. No one knew exactly how her mother had died. Most people said it was from a bad drug interaction with other medication. Caroline never corrected them. That it caused her heart to stop. Hiding it saved her from the questions. Caroline didn't have to answer people when they made assumptions on their own. So drug interactions became the reason for her mother's death. It was simpler. Easier to explain away.

"I don't know if I can talk about it here," Caroline said as she looked around the bustling coffee shop. Everything inside her gave her the fight or flight response. She felt trapped, unstable, and so *so* scared of everything around her. The world had become her enemy and sometimes it hurt so much to be a part of it, but, for her at least, that had never meant that she wanted to die. It just meant that she wanted the fear to go away. She was more afraid of dying than she ever was of living.

"Want to go out to my car?" Bennett asked, squeezing her hand lightly.

Caroline couldn't tell him no. He deserved an answer. So, she agreed and he led her outside, her full cup of coffee still on the table.

When they sat down in the car, Bennett turned on the heater, trying to warm them both up. The chill made Caroline want to retreat further into herself, but she couldn't. She had to get him to go to Florida with her and in order to do that, he needed the truth.

So, she tried to begin. She tried to tell the single most painful story of her whole entire life.

It had happened nearly seven months ago. She remembered her mother being prescribed antibiotics for a cold that turned into bronchitis. Caroline remembered it being her birthday. Her mother had woken her up with a stack of pancakes that smelled like fresh fruit and sugar. There had been a small candle in the middle that Caroline blew out with ease.

She had wished for an acceptance letter from FSU.

When her mother had asked her to stay in to watch movies—saying that she had a surprise gift that she wanted to give to her—Caroline had politely declined. She had wanted to go out with Izzy. They were going to go to a bar for the first time ever.

Caroline never got to open her present.

She remembered opening the door to her house when she got back. The lights were off. The windows were open. Candles were almost burnt down to the wick all around the house. It smelled like hot chocolate and smoke and a variety of fall scents that came from the candles.

Caroline had called her mother's name as she walked into the house. It was cold. Unusually cold for that time of year. So, she closed all the windows. She blew out the candles and turned on the lights. When she went into the kitchen, she screamed.

She had screamed. Screamed. Screamed.

You're alone.

Her mother was laying on the floor, mouth open, hands around her own throat. Her lips were blue. Her eyes were staring at the ceiling.

Caroline screamed her mother's name. She shook her shoulders. Tried to pry her mother's stiff hands away from her neck. She hit her mother's chest. Begged her to breathe.

Breathe.

She had called 911 as she cried. The phone had been just out of her mother's reach. *Fix it.* Caroline had vaguely remembered learning CPR and tried so hard to bring her back. She had pleaded with her mother not to die. *You're going to die.*

The seams of her entire world had unraveled that night and she still had never found a way to patch them back together. Not then. Not now even after months of therapy. She was still broken and she often wondered if she'd just always be that way.

In the end, all she was able to say to Bennett was "I found her when I came home. It was my birthday. She was already blue. She had an allergic reaction. They think it was the medicine." With those few words, she felt the world around her begin to spin. She had never said it out loud, what had happened. She knew that she had barely told Bennett anything, but it was more than she had ever told anyone else. Her lungs were seizing and she felt on the verge of breaking. It was that same feeling of darkness that meant she was about to die. Everything was cold and her hands began to shake. *Breathe.*

"Caroline, breathe," she heard Bennett say. He was holding her face. "Look at me, Caro."

She looked up at him and began counting her breaths.

One. Two. Three. Four.

Caroline stared at his eyes, watching him as he watched her. She felt him breathe with her. Felt his chest rise and fall with his hands as he held her. Tears were streaming down her cheeks. She tried to wipe them away, but he wouldn't let her.

"It's okay to cry, Caroline."

She took a deep, shuttering breath and felt the tears go even faster. "She's dead," Caroline croaked. "She left me alone. I'm all alone." That was when the sobs pierced her throat.

Bennett pulled her to his chest and held her as she cried. It felt better that way: to cry while being held. It felt less dangerous. Less isolating. "You're not alone," he whispered into her ear.

Those words calmed her tears as she breathed him in. She wasn't alone. No matter if she was mad at her grandparents or at Izzy. She had them still. She had Bennett. She was not alone.

"It makes sense now," Bennett started, "that you hate medication. That you always read the warning labels. That you are terrified of dying alone." He was petting her hair as she rested her face against him.

"Sometimes I try to remember what it felt like before she died," Caroline whispered. "I'm starting to forget. I don't even know what normal is anymore." She stayed quiet for a long time, wondering how she had fallen so far from the person she used to be.

"Caroline Marie Rolland," Bennett said as he tucked a stray strand of hair behind her ear after she had finally pulled away from him. He took in a deep breath and pushed his glasses back up the bridge of his nose.

"That's my name," Caroline said with a smile, trying to find meaning in his words.

Bennett shook his head. "Yes, but no. Those were my words."

She looked at him confusedly.

"When Mrs. Ramirez asked us to pick three words that represented who our classmates were as people using the beginning of each of our names, I couldn't think of anything to put for you. There were no three words to describe you and I was just so—" Bennett laughed quietly as he looked down at his lap. "I'm never speechless. Words seem to be the one thing that I'm good at using. At least when I'm writing, that is. And for this dumb project I couldn't think of three words to describe you. So, I wrote your name because that seemed to be the only thing that would encompass you and all of you."

Caroline thought back then to the paper she received with all of her classmates complimentary words. Somehow, she had imagined that Bennett wrote each one of them even though she knew it was from several different people. She remembered seeing her name written on her paper and she was so confused. She had thought that someone obviously didn't understand the assignment. But what she had mistaken for negligence was actually Bennett's attempt of trying to make her see that the only thing fit enough to describe her was her own name. Herself.

"Benevolent," Caroline said as she smiled at him.

The corners of his mouth twitched and it made Caroline blush to see the happiness spread across his face so quickly.

"What about the rest?" he asked.

Caroline thought quickly of the reason she had asked him to come to coffee. "So, to get the rest of your name," Caroline started, "you need to do something for me."

His eyebrows raised over the frame of his glasses. "And what's that exactly?"

Caroline looked down at her lap and whispered, "I need you to come with me to Florida."

"What did you say?"

"I need you to come with me to Florida."

Somehow, Bennett's eyebrows rose higher. "Florida?" he asked, and then recognition flooded his face. "For the tour."

Caroline nodded.

"Izzy and your grandparents didn't want to go?"

His question hurt her even though she knew he wasn't trying to insult her. But she knew he was asking because they knew her better and they were the most logical choices. "I want *you* to come," she said.

"Because you're mad at them?" he asked. "Or because you don't want them telling you that FSU is where you want to be?"

"Bennett," she started, "you make me feel safe. And, yes, there is a part of me that wants to be spiteful and not ask them because I'm mad at them, but there's a bigger part of me that wants *you* there instead because I think we'd have fun. I want to spend time with you Bennett. I want to… I want to be with you."

Bennett blushed and Caroline would have dissolved into a fit of giggles had it not been for the fact that she was trying to be so serious.

She smiled at him again as she reached over to touch his cheek. "I want to be with you, Benevolent Bennett."

Bennett laughed. "It sounds like I'm a knight."

"You wish you were a knight," Caroline smiled back, still holding his cheek as she pulled him close to kiss him. This time, though, she kissed him for the right reasons. Not because she was overcome by emotions. Not because she wanted to forget what she was feeling. She kissed him because she wanted to remember what she was feeling for once. She kissed him because he was Bennett. And he kissed her back.

They were both smiling into the kiss, pulling each other closer even though there wasn't any possible way they could've gotten closer while kissing. Caroline held his cheeks when she pulled away from his lips, resting her forehead against his forehead.

"Please come with me, Bennett. Come on an adventure with me."

Bennett reached up and brushed his thumb against her bottom lip. It made her whole body tingle. "I have one condition."

Caroline smiled. "Besides getting to hear the words I picked out for your name?"

He nodded and pulled a little further away from her face. "You have to bring your medicine with you."

Caroline's stomach dropped. After telling him that her mom died from an allergic reaction to medication, he wanted her to *take* it?

"You don't have to take it, Caro. Just keep it with you in case you need it."

She thought about it for a moment. She had told Dr. B that they could talk about the medication. Her grandmother had told her that she had to start taking the pills. But she wasn't sure she would have to do either. Now? Bennett saying this was his one stipulation? Caroline couldn't deny him that. It wasn't like she ever had to take them. She just had to… take them.

"Okay," she said. "Okay, I will."

Bennett breathed out a sigh of relief that Caroline wondered if he had been holding in that whole time since they met in the booth inside the coffee shop. "Thank you," he said. "Thank you."

They were both silent after that. Caroline couldn't imagine that her simply bringing her medicine was enough to warrant the thanks that he gave her, but then again, she hadn't gone through what he had with his brother.

They were going to board their flight to Florida in three days. Grams had gone into overdrive making sure that everything was booked, that no questions could have been asked, and that Caroline had no chance to ever back out or make an excuse not to go in only two days. She had even already talked to the school to make sure that Caroline had an excuse for missing. When her Grams had asked Caroline who was going with her, she had said Bennett's name before even talking to him about it. Somehow with Grams' adult secrets, she either talked to Bennett's parents or already knew enough about him to buy the ticket.

Caroline and Bennett would be there from Thursday to Sunday and Caroline found it so nerve-racking to think of being that far from home for that long when she could hardly go to her backyard by herself. She had to believe that she'd be okay, though, because if she couldn't be okay, where would that leave her? What would she do? Where would she go then?

Chapter 15

Caroline was packing her bags Wednesday night when she heard a light knock on her door. She prayed that it wasn't her grandmother because she didn't think she'd be able to face her after giving her the silent treatment for so long. Especially if she asked Caroline direct questions (which—of course—Caroline would have to answer to avoid being completely disrespectful). Because the truth was, even though she was mad at her grandmother, it wasn't so bad that she'd completely disrespect her and make her upset no matter how badly Caroline may have wanted to retaliate.

"Kiddo?" It was her gramps. "Can I come in?"

With the war—or rather the complete lack of interaction—going on between Grams and Caroline, Gramps had been staying safely on the sidelines. It would've been mildly adorable that her gramps was so averse to emotions if Caroline hadn't been the one feeling those emotions.

"Sure," she told him since he had just been waiting in the doorway.

Gramps walked in slowly as Caroline was sitting on the floor, clothes all around her, and an open suitcase to her left. He closed the door behind him and went to sit on Caroline's bed.

"I know you've been having a tough time lately," he started slowly.

Caroline didn't want to meet his eyes. She didn't want to see him pleading with her through his features, his wrinkles more defined with his frown. She just wanted to be able to stare at the floor pretending to decide which pair of shorts to bring.

"Do you want to talk about it?" he asked.

Caroline shook her head, not trusting her voice. She wasn't sure why she was this emotional. It seemed like Gramps was the last one on her side and he was trying so hard to play the mediator between her and her grandmother.

"Okay, then I will just talk for a while...." he said and trailed off. He stayed silent for a long moment before continuing. "We sold your mother's house."

The lump returned in Caroline's throat. She didn't know what to do because she definitely could not look up at him now no matter how much she wanted to. Her childhood home? Or at least, the only childhood home she remembered. The home she was raised in for the first seven years of her life was in Florida.

Caroline decided to throw a random article of clothing into her suitcase. "Oh yeah?" she asked, trying to feign nonchalance.

"Yeah," her grandfather said softly. "We're hiring some people to box up your mother's things, but I think I'll go over there and just—"

Gramps never ended up finishing his sentence. He just sat there, hanging in the middle of a sentence, as if the world would stop with him.

"Do you think they can get it done before I come back?" Caroline asked still desperately trying not to turn around and look at him.

"Yeah, kiddo, I think they can do that. There's not that much left anyway."

Caroline agreed. There wasn't much left of her mother. At least not there. Not in that house. That house didn't feel warm anymore. Not without her in it.

Caroline finally turned around to face her grandfather. There was something she needed to make sure of. "Will you—" Caroline croaked. She cleared her throat and tried not to sound too emotional. "Will you let me know if you find anything? I mean, you know, anything for me."

Gramps knew about the birthday gift that could never be found. Grams did, too. They just didn't know that Caroline had left her own mother alone to die when she had asked Caroline to stay.

Gramps smiled at her sadly and nodded. "Of course." He patted her shoulder gently, and then used her shoulder as a point of balance as he pushed his weight into her shoulder in order to stand. "Your Grams wanted me to give you these," Gramps started as his cheeks flushed. He handed Caroline a grocery bag. "We got them from the pharmacy, so no one saw, but she just wanted to make sure—"

Caroline looked in the grocery bag and saw the condoms. "*Gramps!*" she nearly shrieked. She tried to hand them back to him.

Gramps shook his head and began to back away. "We know you'll be staying in a room with Bennett and we just want you to be smart."

"Gramps, it's not like that—" she said even though she wasn't completely sure that was the truth. She hadn't thought about staying in the room alone with Bennett. It made butterflies flutter in her stomach.

"She'll send me right back if I take those from you. Please don't make me do this again," Gramps said, truly pleading.

Caroline laughed and blushed furiously. She tossed the box of condoms to the side, wanting to forget about the whole thing.

Gramps smiled shyly. "You know your grandmother loves you, right?"

Caroline turned around to see him standing by the door, hand waiting on the doorknob.

"I know," Caroline said despite the anger, embarrassment, and so many other emotions she was still feeling. "I love her, too."

"And I love you. Even more than I love your grandmother's cooking," Gramps said with a smirk.

Caroline laughed—she couldn't help herself—and nodded towards the door to shoo her grandfather away.

When she was left alone, she finished packing except for one thing. One tiny, problem-evoking, potentially-problem-solving thing. The pills. So, she went into her bathroom and looked at the pill bottles all lined up neatly in her medicine cabinet. On the top of each one was something new: dates and numbers of pills. Her grandmother started keeping tabs. It would be easy enough to just throw all of them out. Flush every single one down the toilet. Caroline couldn't do it, though. Whether it was the promise she made Bennett, or the unanswered questions she left for Dr. B about talking about them, she couldn't just throw them away. Even if they scared her more than she cared to admit.

So, she took a bottle and stuffed it away in her bag, knowing that she most likely wouldn't be taking them in Florida, but at least she wasn't breaking her promise. The only thing that left her with was the condoms....

As she looked at the box in her hand, she wanted to puke from her nerves. She couldn't *believe* that her grandfather had given her those. She tossed the box in the corner and closed her bag. All she had to do now was wait. The flight was later in the afternoon the next day. She and Bennett wouldn't get to Florida until nighttime. They'd go straight to the hotel, check in, and then get ready for their tour the next day. Their flight back wasn't scheduled until Sunday, so they had all day Friday and Saturday to explore Florida. Her grandmother had actually told her that she was required to take pictures as proof that they went.

The fact that Gramps and Grams were actually allowing Caroline to take Bennett with her and actually stay in the same hotel room (granted, with two double beds), blew Caroline's mind a bit. She guessed they wanted to feel more responsible by giving her the condoms. It made her wonder, though, if they were trying to give her a little slack to make the FSU trip a little less miserable.

So far, her nerves had been fine, but now that the trip was less than twenty-four hours away, she couldn't keep herself from feeling jittery.

Just as she was beginning to do her breathing exercises, her phone buzzed. When she picked it up and saw who it was from, she couldn't help the huge smile that spread across her face.

THURS – 9:09 PM
Bennett: I bet you can't sleep.

Caroline laughed.

THURS – 9:09 PM
Caroline: I bet you're right.

THURS – 9:10 PM
Bennett: Tomorrow's the day.

THURS – 9:10 PM
Caroline: Yep.

THURS – 9:11 PM
Bennett: Wanna meet me in Utah?

Caroline nearly jumped up from her sitting position on the floor in her bedroom, but ended up falling to the rug instead.

THURS – 9:12 PM
Caroline: Already there.

She began putting on clothes that were warm enough to stay outside as well as socks and her tennis shoes. She grabbed a blanket as her phone buzzed in her hand over and over again.

THURS – 9:12 PM

Bennett: Now, why are you lying to me?
Bennett: I'm literally alone out here.
Bennett: All the way in Utah.

Caroline stopped in her tracks and laughed as she opened her bedroom door and went way faster than was necessary out the back door and into the backyard. There, a few yards in front of her, was Bennett. He was sitting on a blanket and had a huge lump next to him. Caroline smiled, feeling it all the way to her eyes. It was the jacket-blanket.

She went over to him and sat down.

"Now, you do know that this is *my* hiding spot and people aren't allowed to come here without me," Caroline said as she slipped on the jacket-blanket.

Bennett raised his eyebrows as he watched her putting the jacket-blanket on. "Now," he started with a smirk, "you do realize that is *my* jacket and people aren't allowed to use it without my permission."

Caroline took it off and handed it to him. She scootched to where her back was facing him. "Go on then," she said cockily as she stuck her arms out wide, forming a T.

He pushed his glasses up the bridge of his nose and laughed nervously. He slipped the jacket-blanket on her shoulders and was about to pull away from her when she turned her head quickly to kiss him. When she pulled away, she watched as he looked down nervously, still unsure of how to act around her. She reached up to touch his face, rubbing her thumb gently across his cheek.

"Thank you," she said, "for going with me tomorrow. I know it may not be the ideal weekend, but—"

"It's a good weekend if I get to get out of Arizona," he said. "Especially if I get to spend that weekend with you."

Caroline felt all of her tumultuous feelings rise to the surface again. Everything that made her feel so uncertain. Everything that made her feel as if her emotions had nowhere to go. As if they had to stay bottled up in her forever, threatening to explode.

"What if... what if I can't be okay?" Caroline murmured. "What if this trip just makes everything worse?"

Bennett was silent for a long time. They ended up both looking up at the stars. It made her feel so small and large at the same time. "Then we keep going. You and me. Because we can make it better. You, me, Izzy, your gramps and grams: we can make it better." He turned to her and held her face in his hands. "We keep going," he said in an almost pleading tone.

Caroline nodded. "We keep going." She wondered how much pain was hiding behind those words. She wondered how much his brother's, Josh's, death had really affected him. Because the longer and longer she stayed with him—the closer she got—the more she noticed the cracks. The ones that looked so much like her own.

Keep going.

Fix it.
We keep going.

Chapter 16

As if the trip itself weren't torture enough, Caroline was actually forced to go to school the next morning. It had honestly really sucked because she had been trying to avoid her yearbook teacher. Like the horrible editor she was, she still hadn't come up with a theme for the yearbook. So, when he asked her if she had any ideas and she told him no, she wasn't surprised when he told her she had by the beginning of next week to come up with something or he would be forced to let a junior come up with an idea instead.

So, yeah, on top of that horrible beginning to the day, Caroline's nerves were on overdrive and she couldn't stop herself from fidgeting every second of every moment. She tried to occupy herself after school because she still had nearly two hours before they needed to get to the airport but nothing worked. Absolutely *nothing*.

Caroline paced and checked her phone (three times) and fixed her makeup (two times) *and* opened the pantry for snacks (four times) that she couldn't even find the appetite to eat.

"Caroline," her grams called after watching her get up for the umpteenth time. "Sit still, I have something for you. I'll be right back."

Right. Sit still. She could do that.

When her grams returned, there was a look in her eyes that Caroline couldn't quite place. "I wanted you to remember why you wanted to go to Florida State in the first place. I want you to go on this trip and *have fun*. I want you, Caroline, to remember everything that you've worked so hard to achieve and everything you've done to get to where you are now." Grams came close to Caroline and held her hand. She turned Caroline's palm up and placed a piece of thick paper in her palm.

It was a picture.

When Caroline turned it over, she saw her mom and dad. They were picnicking on the Landis Green. There was a secret laugh between them, a joke that no one would ever know. It was her parents. Both of her dead parents.

But it was her parents who made her want to go to FSU in the first place. It wasn't them forcing her. It wasn't them saying that FSU was the best college for her. It was the way her mother talked about the college. It was the way her eyes had always sparkled when she mentioned the campus as if she were talking about a storybook land. It was the fact that FSU was where her parents met. Caroline grew up believing that FSU was magical, and in some weird way, she had grown up to think that FSU would give her that happily ever after she had been searching for.

"They would want you to go. They wouldn't want you holding yourself back because of what happened to them."

Caroline stared at the picture. She stared at the fairytale land and the people she believed to be the king and queen of the kingdom. She loved them both so much and they were both gone. How was she supposed to find that magic without them?

"I love you, Caroline," her grams said.

Caroline looked up at her grams and felt the fear bubbling in the pit of her stomach. "I love you, too, Grams," Caroline said, feeling choked.

"Hey!" Bennett called cheerily as he walked in the door. "Ready to go?"

Caroline looked at her grams, looked over to see her gramps observing them, and stood up. She hugged them both and turned to Bennett, trying to hide her shaking hands. "Ready."

***

The airport was an absolute *disaster*. It wasn't like it was Caroline's first time taking a flight. She and her mother had travelled a few times before she died. Somehow, though, with her nerves threatening to steal her breath, the airport was ten times worse than she remembered it.

There were so many people. All of them pushing and shoving and trying to get to where they needed to be. Bennett was holding her hand and she vaguely registered that he was saying something to her. She just couldn't get her brain to work for long enough to understand what he was saying. She felt trapped and surrounded and way too overwhelmed. Her ears were ringing and her fingers and toes were beginning to tingle, signaling to her that she needed to fix it. Fast.

Breathe.

Fix it.

"Caroline," Bennett said, grabbing her by both of her shoulders. "Look at me. I'm here."

She looked at him and the world came back into focus. She breathed with him.

"We're just going to get in line at security and wait to go through. Then, all we have to do is find our gate and sit tight. We can do this. *You* can do this. It's just you and me." He took her hand again and led her in the direction of security.

The line was horrendously long, but Caroline focused all of her energy on feeling Bennett's hand in her own. When it was time for them to put their stuff on the conveyor belt and go through the scanner, Caroline felt slightly better.

"Hey, kid," the security guard called to her.

Caroline felt her whole body freeze as she turned to face the older man.

"It's okay to smile," he said as he smiled kindly at her.

"We don't bite," the female security guard said as she came up next to the both of them, a soft smile on her face.

Caroline laughed nervously and made a concentrated effort to smile at them both as she stepped into the machine and put her hands above her head. They sent her on her way. She grabbed her bags and met Bennett on the other side.

"Okay?" Bennett asked as he grabbed her hand softly again.

Caroline nodded and took a deep breath. "Okay."

They walked to their boarding gate, passing the hundreds of people rushing around them. Airports were funny like that. Everyone always seemed to be rushing and anxious. Just like her every day of her life, she guessed.

Bennett took them to two empty seats and they set their bags down. Caroline felt a little weight fall off of her shoulders as she sat down. They were here. The plane was boarding in another hour and a half. They were where they needed to be.

Her stomach growled. It was almost four o'clock and she hadn't eaten lunch. Caroline looked back out to the buzzing airport. She wasn't sure if she was willing to risk another trip into that crowd just for food. As if reading her thoughts, her stomach growled again, more insistent this time.

Bennett looked down at her and smiled with his eyebrows raised. "Hungry?"

"No," Caroline said as she shook her head. But her stomach growled *again*. The damn thing. Giving her away like that.

He laughed. "I can go get us some food?"

As he began to stand, Caroline grabbed onto his arm. She wasn't sure if she could be alone. Not feeling so unstable and stormy.

Bennett nodded at her, understanding her pleading eyes without having to ask what was wrong. He stood up straight and looked around them. "There," he pointed to a place a few yards away from them. It was a little sushi place that was close enough for Caroline to see everyone waiting in line. "I can go there and get us some food. You'll be able to see me the whole time. You just need to sit here and watch our bags."

Before she could say anything, he walked away. No less than ten seconds later, though, he turned abruptly around and started walking back towards her.

"Do you even like sushi?" he asked, his face scrunched up in an adorable look of disorientation. He pushed his glasses back up the bridge of his nose.

Caroline felt the laugh bubble out of her before she had the chance to even think about it. He was just so... adorable. She couldn't help herself. "Nothing raw," she said. "But, yes, I love sushi."

Bennett gave her a half-smile as he nodded and walked back to the sushi restaurant to get in line.

It was a long wait, but it wasn't a terrible one. Every now and then, Bennett would look over to her and give her two thumbs up. She'd smile and nod at him, making sure that he knew she was okay. Having him in eyesight worked out well. Her nerves stayed under control and she never felt like she was sinking.

While waiting, her grams texted her to make sure she was okay. She responded that everything was going great (a small fib, but she wanted to prove to her grams that she was fine). Caroline knew that when she got back to Arizona, her grandparents would want to know everything. She had to make sure that everything she told them was positive. She had to make sure that they understood that she loved FSU, but it wasn't as great as she thought it would be. She *had* to make sure they knew that she wanted to stay in Arizona. Because there was one thing she knew for sure: she wouldn't have been able to do this had Bennett not come with her.

"Dinner is served," Bennett said as he sat down next to her, handing her a plastic to-go plate with an assortment of fried sushi in it.

Caroline was so hungry that it almost hurt. Sitting on the chair was awkward because there weren't any tables next to them, so she ended up moving to the floor. She sat cross-legged with the sushi in front of her. Caroline opened up the plastic plate and the smell hit her. It smelled absolutely heavenly. She made a little set up on the lid of her to-go plate with spicy mayo and soy sauce and went to work.

Bennett came to sit on the floor next to her. She tried to eat slowly so she didn't look completely ridiculous in front of him, but it was just *so* good that she couldn't help herself from eating piece after piece, hardly stopping to take a breath.

"Just a little FYI," Bennett said slowly, a smile creeping up his cheeks. "I don't know the Heimlich maneuver, so please don't choke."

Caroline stopped eating just to glare at him. "Ha ha," she said, swallowing the piece of sushi in her mouth. "Very funny."

He laughed and Caroline laughed with him. She felt way more at ease now that she had food in her stomach and they were settled at their boarding gate. It felt almost fun. Almost.

When they were done eating, they both got back up and Bennett took all their trash to throw it away. Caroline sank back into her chair and began sorting colors on her phone. It wasn't that she needed it to take her mind off her nerves, it was more that she had done it for so long now that it was almost routine. She found it almost sad that something she used as a safety blanket had become routine for her. It left such a bad taste in her mouth that she closed the app. The problem with closing the app, though, was that she didn't have anything else to do. At least they'd start boarding soon. Well, in forty-five minutes they would.

"The waiting has got to be the worst part," Bennett said as he held his hand politely in his lap. "Going back and forth from Massachusetts was horrible."

"Did you really come back that often?" Caroline asked. She never really remembered hearing about him coming back to Arizona. Not after his brother died. He kind of just went to college and never came back.

Bennett laughed as he looked down at his lap. "No, not really. But when I *did* come back, waiting in the airport was the worst."

Caroline smiled at him and watched as he began fidgeting more with his fingers. She reached over and grabbed his hand. She wasn't sure why she did it exactly, she just wanted to hold his hand. She hadn't gotten to enjoy it earlier when she was freaking out about all the people and going through security.

It was funny the way that their relationship had developed. Caroline wasn't even truly sure what they were. They had never defined it, but they had held hands. They had kissed. Did that make them a couple? Was he her boyfriend? They really hadn't talked about it and it was starting to irk Caroline. Not to mention they were going to be sleeping in the same hotel room that night. That thought alone made her stomach do somersaults.

"So, you'll be starting your junior year of college in the fall?" Caroline asked him.

"Well, technically my sophomore year since I took a year off for internships."

"Right," Caroline said. "Are internships good for law school?"

"Yes, if you get the really good ones..." Bennet said as he trailed off. "To be honest, though, Caro, it was the only way my dad would let me take a year off."

"You didn't want to do the internship?"

"Not really." Bennett pushed his glasses back up the bridge of his nose. Caroline wanted him to look at her while he talked. She wanted him to stop looking so... trapped.

"What did you want to do?"

"Don't laugh," he smiled, still staring at his lap.

"Literally, Bennett, I would *never*," she said as she smiled at him. She bent her head over to try and look at his face as his head hung down. His eyes met hers and she smiled brighter as they both sat up straighter.

"I wanted to take a year off to write," he said. He laughed nervously. "I love writing. I always have."

Caroline stopped smiling. She was confused as she thought about it for a little while. "Then why not go into writing?"

"Well, as a lawyer I get to major in English, so I'm taking a lot of the same classes."

"Yeah but you're going into *law*. That's not the same thing."

Bennett began fidgeting again, so Caroline started rubbing circles on the back of his hand with her thumb like he always did to keep her calm. He remained quiet.

"It makes sense now that I think about it," Caroline started. "You quoting famous writers. Sounding so romantic all the time."

She watched as Bennett's cheeks turned a dark shade of red. It made her feel good to know she had that effect on him. She loved his warm, coffee-colored skin. It made her want to hold him just to feel his warmth.

"Romantic, huh?"

"Don't change the subject, Bennett," Caroline said in a mock chastising tone.

He chuckled darkly. "Law has never really been my thing."

Caroline looked at him questioningly. "Then whose thing is it?"

"Josh's," Bennett said quietly.

And that one name broke her heart for Bennett because it told her so much about him without hardly telling her anything at all. "Bennett..." she started.

"Good afternoon passengers. This is the pre-boarding announcement for flight 87B to Tallahassee, Florida. We are now inviting those passengers with small children—and any passengers requiring special assistance—to begin boarding at this time."

Caroline looked over to the boarding gate and back over to Bennett. "We'll continue this conversation later," she said, pointing at him menacingly and hoping that it would lighten his mood.

He gave her a small smile and Caroline decided that was enough for her.

It didn't take long after that for them to begin boarding the flight. When they finally got onto the airplane and into their seats, Caroline was lucky enough to have a window seat assigned to her. Poor Bennett had the middle seat with an older woman right next to him. That wasn't the worst part, though. The older woman had a small Pomeranian on her lap that looked as if it would like to bite both Bennett and Caroline.

They exchanged fearful glances, and then laughed together. It was going to be a *long* flight.

Chapter 17

The whole plane was dark. The flight attendants had turned the lights off to let those who wanted to sleep get a nap in. The flight itself was around four hours and thirty minutes. Since they left around five thirty, they weren't going to get into Florida until ten, but that also didn't account for them losing two hours. So in Florida, it would be midnight by the time they landed. Miserable, if you asked Caroline, but it was one of the only flights that worked with their schedules.

All she was doing was staring out the window. All she could see was darkness and the occasional cloud, but all she could *hear* was the older lady snoring next to them. The Pomeranian was sitting protectively on her lap, waiting for either Caroline or Bennett to make a wrong move. She thought Bennett was sleeping, but she heard him rustling beside her.

He leaned over and whispered in her ear, "I'm scared this dog is going to eat me."

Caroline tried to suppress her laughter as much as she could to be respectful to the sleeping passengers. The dog growled, low and guttural, in response to Caroline's giggles. It made her want to laugh even more.

"What are you thinking about?" he asked her once they both settled back down.

Caroline watched a flight attendant walk studiously down the aisle of the plane, checking on each of the passengers. "Honestly? Nothing. My mind has been blank this whole flight."

Bennett looked at her curiously. "I've just been thinking about this trip. About you. About my brother. About my future." The last one came a little softer than the first three. Caroline had a feeling that she knew why.

"About college?"

"Yeah."

"Why'd you go into a field that you never wanted to be in?" Caroline asked. She had her seat leaned back and her legs curled up into the seat.

Bennett sighed. "It's a really—" he stopped himself. "It's just a really long story."

"Did you really mean it when you said we could fix it together?"

"Of course I did, Caro," he said softly, tucking a stray strand of her hair away from her face.

"Maybe then," she started slowly, "we can help to fix each other." She knew what she was implying when she said that. She knew that it meant that he was broken, too. But something in her told her that Bennett was hurting almost the same—if not more— than Caroline.

Bennett reached over and grabbed Caroline's hand, holding it tightly as if he were going to fall. Caroline gripped his hand back, letting him know that she was there for him in the same way that he had let her know the same so many times already.

"What are we, Bennett?" Caroline asked. Her intense need to know finally got the best of her. She had to ask him and she hoped that it would be an answer she liked.

"What do you mean?" he asked, sitting up a little straighter.

"We've been hanging out for a few weeks now. We've been on a couple dates. I've kissed you." She glanced over to him. "More than once, I might add," she mumbled. "And I just—I don't know where we stand. Where we *will* stand in the future. If you even want there to be a future."

"Are you saying you want a future with me?" Bennett asked nervously.

"Are *you* saying you want a future with me?" Caroline parroted with an uneasy smile.

Bennett laughed and had to quiet himself. "Caroline," he started just with her name. "Caroline, I've wanted you to be my girlfriend ever since we had that art class together with Mrs. Ramirez. I've just never had the guts to ask."

"You can ask me now... or... I can ask you?" Caroline offered sheepishly.

Bennett smiled. "Do you want to go out with me? I mean, do you want to be my girl? Girlfriend, I mean." Bennett was stumbling over his words and Caroline had to put him out of his misery.

"Of course, Benevolent Bennett," she giggled. She reached her hand up to hold his cheek. He felt warm under her palm. "Of course," she whispered as she leaned in to kiss him.

The Pomeranian began growling again, but Caroline didn't pay it much attention.

"My dog doesn't like that," the older lady said.

Caroline and Bennett nearly jumped apart. When Caroline looked over to the woman, her eyes were still closed. She looked over at Bennett, who looked just as puzzled as she was. Then, they laughed whole-heartedly. It was hard to suppress the laughter even after several people shushed them.

**

It was late when the plane finally landed and they were able to get through the airport. It had taken an obscenely long time for their ride to get there, and when they were finally dropped off at the hotel, Caroline was exhausted. It was past one in the morning in Florida, and even though she often spent her nights staring at the ceiling, traveling had taken so much energy out of her.

When Caroline looked up at the hotel they were supposed to be staying in, she was surprised by how nice it looked. She didn't know that this place was in her grandparents budget. They had even paid for Bennett's plane ticket.

The hotel was bright despite the time of night. It felt huge and extravagant and almost like the fairytale that Caroline had imagined when she thought of going to college as a child. She and Bennett wheeled their bags up to the check-in desk.

"Caroline Roland," she told the front desk clerk. The poor girl looked just as exhausted as Caroline felt. She wondered how much longer the girl was going to be working that night.

"Here you go, miss Roland," the girl said, handing Caroline a card key. "Breakfast will be served from six tomorrow morning until ten thirty."

"Thank you," Caroline nodded as she and Bennett made their way to the elevator. They were in room 331 on the third floor.

She and Bennett were both silent on the elevator ride up. Caroline could just imagine what she looked like after the day she had and just wanted to hop in the shower and go to bed. Bennett looked as if he wanted the same thing.

When they got in the room, Caroline put her bags next to the bed closest to the door. Bennett put all his things next to the other bed.

"Mind if I shower first?" Caroline asked.

Bennett shook his head. "Not at all."

So, Caroline went to open her bag, and as if it were shoved haphazardly in there in a rush, the condom box popped out and onto the bed. Caroline was *mortified*. She tried her best to hide them before Bennett saw, but it was no use. She made more of a ruckus trying to hide them than she would have if she had remained calm. When he looked over to see the box in her hands, Caroline quickly put the box behind her back, blushing wildly. Bennett's blush mirrored her own.

"It's not what you—" Caroline stammered. "I mean, this isn't what—" she tried again. Then she just threw the condom box on the bed and sank face first into the pillows. "Oh, God," she mumbled into the sheets. "My. Freaking. Grandparents."

She heard Bennett move beside her. He poked her shoulder gently. "Caroline?"

"Just go away," she groaned into the pillows.

"What?"

Caroline flipped over like a fish, hiding her eyes with her arms. "I said, just go away."

"Is that—" Bennett started nervously. Caroline peeked through her arms and saw Bennett staring at the box of condoms. "Is that something that you wanted?"

She wanted to die.

Right there.

She was going to yell at her grandparents so much when she got home that they wouldn't know what hit them. "No!" Caroline said as she bolted upright. "I mean, maybe," she started, waving her hands around wildly, "but not now! It was my grandparents." She groaned again, falling back to the pillows. "I'm going to die right here, right now."

Bennett laughed nervously as he laid down beside her, both of them staring up at the ceiling. "It's nice that they care so much about you," he said.

Caroline sighed loudly. "Too much, if you ask me." She rolled over on her side to face him. "I want to make sure you understand that I don't expect anything and it's still way too early for this and I'm not—" She was rambling, she knew.

"Caroline," Bennett interrupted, rolling over on his side to face her. "I would never expect that of you. I know your grandparents just wanted you to be safe, but I agree with you. I think it's too early for that now," he started, but then began to stumble over his words. "Not that I don't want to either, it's just—"

Caroline laughed, covering her face again. "We are so awkward."

Bennett laughed with her, and then Caroline scooted closer to him to give him a small kiss. His eyelids were drooping and she was beginning to feel extremely tired as well.

"I'll go hurry up and take my shower now," she whispered.

He nodded sleepily and she got up, left the condom box where it was laying on the bed, and got her things together to go to take a shower. She made sure not to take too long so that Bennett wouldn't have to wait.

When she came out, though, he was sleeping on her bed on top of the sheets where she had left him. She smiled as she watched how peaceful he was and went over to take his glasses off. She sat them on the nightstand that the two beds shared, and then rummaged in the closet for an extra blanket. She laid it on top of him and tried not to laugh as his mouth fell open in his sleep.

She went over to the empty bed, got in the covers, and thought about all of the things that would happen tomorrow. It was daunting, to say the least, imagining finally getting to visit the college of her dreams but still knowing that she would never attend. She rolled onto her side to watch Bennett sleep. He still looked exhausted—even while sleeping—as he laid on the bed opposite of her. It made her smile even as she began to dread the tour tomorrow.

Her thoughts wound around in her head like that for a long time. Her brain refused to shut off, but she was so used to that by now. Tomorrow was the tour. It was the first place that they were going after lunch, and the tour was supposed to last for two hours, so they'd be done way before dinner. Maybe they could have their picnic tomorrow after the tour?

At some point, as if no time had passed, Caroline jolted awake to the sound of the door.

"Sorry," Bennett said with a smile. He was holding two plates of food and daylight was coming in through the curtains. "I didn't mean to wake you. Breakfast was going to end soon and I knew we'd need some food, so I just, you know." Bennett shrugged and smiled at her goofily. His hair looked wet as if he had woken up and taken a shower.

Caroline was still a little dazed and confused, looking at her phone for the time, and then outside at the light blinding her.

"What time is it?"

"Almost eleven," Bennett said as he set the food down on the table in the corner. "They were getting ready to clean everything up when I went down to get food."

She sat up and rubbed her eyes, her oversized sweatshirt making her feel like an Oompa Loompa. "Did you get waffles?"

Bennett chuckled. "We'll have to wake up a little earlier tomorrow for those. We got the scraps."

Caroline pouted childishly and knew that she probably looked ridiculous, but she didn't care.

Bennett came over to her bed and sat down on the side of it. "Tomorrow," he said, "I will get you your waffles."

"Promise?"

"Promise," he said as he took her hand and led her out of the bed.

"I'm just *so* tired," she grumbled. "Maybe we should skip the tour today."

Bennett raised his eyebrows and gave her a chastising glance.

She threw her hands up. "I know, I know. I was only kidding," she said as Bennett gave her a sidelong look. "Mostly."

"Do you have any idea what you want to do on this trip?" Bennett asked as he took a bite of his eggs.

Caroline took a bite of her own. They were cold. Definitely the scraps. "I have a list," she said as she picked through her food. Her nerves were starting to get the best of her.

"Can I see it?"

So, she stood up and rummaged through her bag for the folded up list she had made a few days ago on the café napkin. "Here," she said as she handed it to Bennett.

He slowly unfolded it and read aloud. "Tour campus, sad face," he read. "Why does it have a sad face?"

Caroline waved him off. "Just keep going."

"Go to the Sweet Shop where Mom and Dad met. That one should be pretty easy." His eyes scanned down the list. "Picnic at Landis Green—we can do that one today."

She nodded in agreement.

"Go to the beach," he cringed.

"What? What is wrong with going to the beach? We're in *Florida*."

Bennett paused as he looked at the ceiling and pushed his glasses back up the bridge of his nose. "I didn't bring a swimsuit."

"*What?!*" Caroline nearly shouted in indignation. "You didn't bring a *swimsuit* to *Florida*?"

"Okay, okay," Bennett resigned. "I know, not smart on my part."

Caroline shook her head, acting disappointed in him. "Keep going."

"Feed the seagulls," Bennett said. "You're not very original with this are you?"

"Hey!" Caroline laughed as she lightly punched him on his shoulder.

"Don't think," Bennett said as his eyebrows knitted together.

She was confused for a moment as to what he was trying to tell her, but then remembered that it was on her list. Oh. She had forgotten that was there. It made her deflate a bit.

"Well," Bennett started slowly, "I think we can get all of these done. Except the last one."

Caroline looked over to him, confused.

"You'll be having so much fun that you won't be able to stop thinking about it. It'll be the good thoughts that you can't get rid of."

She smiled, feeling so grateful for him in that moment. "I think that sounds great."

Chapter 18

Things to do with Bennett in Florida:
1. Tour campus :(

They packed lunch for the campus tour and a blanket to use for their picnic. What Caroline hadn't anticipated was the sheer amount of walking that they'd be doing. She had *seriously* underestimated the size of FSU's campus. There were a lot of things she had underestimated....

For starters, she had underestimated how beautiful the campus was. Their tour guide highlighted so many parts of campus that Caroline hadn't known about. She was sure that they were supposed to show all students these landmarks, but it seemed as if their tour guide did it just for them. Their tour guide was an energetic girl wearing a khaki skirt and white tennis shoes with her FSU polo. She had bangs across her forehead with her ponytail pulled high on top of her head. Her gold-rimmed glasses were absurdly oversized on her face, but Caroline thought it added to the girl's personality. Caroline thought her name was Sara, but she wasn't one hundred percent sure.

"FSU is one of the only colleges in the US with a circus on campus," presumably-Sara had said. "What do you want to major in?"

"O-oh," Caroline stammered, surprised by the question. She wasn't sure how to answer that. She didn't know how to tell the girl standing in front of her—or Bennett, for that matter—that she had always wanted to be a pharmacist. She wanted to be like her grandparents. She wanted to make them proud. Even more since her mother had died. She wanted to make sure that it wouldn't happen to anyone else. She wanted to develop medicine without side effects that killed people. She couldn't exactly say *all* of that, though. So, she simply said, "I want to be a pharmacist," and they continued on their tour as if the question hadn't completely thrown Caroline off. Although, Bennett did give her a pretty curious side glance.

Caroline was amazed. She had to consciously close her mouth several times (especially after the circus, the Sweet Shop, and the union). She loved the Strozier Library and could imagine herself studying for exams there while drinking a coffee. Caroline could imagine her mother going to each of these places—except, of course, the newly made union. She thought of her mother and father meeting on this campus. She thought of them waiting for class at the Landis Green. She thought of them staying in dorms and eating the cafeteria food. She thought of all of the things they could have done together and wished that she could do each of those things, too.

She underestimated how hard it would be to say no to this place.

After nearly two hours of walking, the tour was over. Bennett led her to the Landis Green where they began to set up their picnic. Caroline saw many college students and even more dogs. She watched as the students laughed together, as they threw footballs and frisbees, as they laid next to their dogs and looked completely at peace.

When everything was set out, Caroline began to eat. She sat in silence with Bennett as they both ate. All Caroline wanted to do was sit there forever, feeling the sun on her skin, the grass beneath her fingers. It was a comfortable seventy-two degrees without a breeze. She loved the warmth.

"So, what did you think?" Bennett asked.

Caroline had been waiting for that question. She knew what she had to do because if she was going to convince her grandparents that she wanted to stay in Arizona, she had to convince Bennett as well.

"It was okay," Caroline started slowly. She took a bite of her sandwich and chewed it in a way that she hoped feigned nonchalance.

Bennett stopped eating and raised his eyebrows. "If I wasn't in Massachusetts, I'd be here," he said. "You're kidding me, right?"

"No," Caroline said. "I expected more."

Bennett looked at her curiously. "That's not what I got from you during that tour."

She shrugged. "I mean, it's a cool campus. There are so many great things. It's just... It's not what I expected," she said again.

"Caroline..." Bennett started, sounding as if he was about to question her again.

"Give me the list," Caroline said.

"What?"

"The list. Give me the list."

Bennett handed over the napkin-list and Caroline crossed out another item.

Things to do with Bennett in Florida:

1. ~~Tour campus :(~~

2. Go to the Sweet Shop (where Mom and Dad met).

3. ~~Picnic at Landis Green.~~

"You still hungry?" Caroline asked with a smile. "I've been dying to try one of the lattes at the Sweet Shop."

Bennett nodded but didn't smile. They packed up their things and began heading in the direction of the Sweet Shop. It didn't take them long to get there, but Caroline's legs were beginning to ache. Her legs weren't used to moving ever since she quit track after her mom died.

Caroline and Bennett ended up sharing a brownie ice cream sundae, and Caroline ordered a latte that had chocolate and raspberry flavoring in it. It was amazing, if Caroline was going to be completely honest. The brownie sundae, though, definitely made her want to go into a sugar coma. Caroline then pulled out the list and scratched out the Sweet Shop as well.

She looked at the short list of things to do with Bennett. There were only three things left and "Don't think" definitely didn't count as one.

It was almost five o'clock, but neither Bennett nor Caroline were hungry after all they had eaten.

"What should we do now?" Caroline asked.

Bennett looked thoughtful for a moment. "Well, we need something to remember this trip. What better way than with FSU merch?"

Caroline felt her stomach flip. If she brought anything back that had "FSU" stamped on it, it definitely wouldn't fit her narrative of not wanting to go there. "Bennett, I—"

"C'mon," he said as he grabbed her hand. "It's on me."

Bennett led Caroline to the bookstore where they began looking at all the various FSU merchandise. Caroline walked around a few times, seeing the logo that she knew so well. It hurt her heart so bad.

"I think you need this," Bennett said as he popped up from around a corner. He was holding a stuffed horse with face paint on it and a saddle. It was Renegade, the campus's mascot without Osceola, the Indian chief who was normally riding the horse. Her mother and father talked about that mascot a lot. Mainly because they were so proud that FSU had gotten permission from the actual Seminole tribe to use Osceola and Renegade as a mascot. The college had even collaborated with the tribe on how to dress Osceola for football games.

Caroline laughed and took the horse from him, holding it to her chest. "When will I ever use this?"

"Who says you need to use it?" Bennett asked as he pushed his glasses up the bridge of his nose. "You just need to be able to look at it. So we can remember this trip, right?"

Caroline nodded slowly. "Right."

"And I think you should get at least one shirt or something with FSU on it."

"Bennett..." Caroline started. "These are super expensive."

"Credit cards are honestly the best," Bennett said without acknowledging Caroline's statement.

"Bennett," Caroline said again.

"Please let me do this for you, Caro," Bennett said as he grabbed her hand.

Caroline relented. She couldn't exactly tell him no after he had asked so nicely. It was adorable seeing him like that. He was so kind and caring and thought of Caroline without making her feel like she was broken or a burden.

She led him over to the sweatshirts and picked out a beautiful heather gray one. When they went to check out, Bennett paid and gave her the bag. After they were out of the checkout line, he bent down cautiously, and then—with more confidence—kissed her on the forehead.

Caroline just closed her eyes and smiled. Everything felt so right. Her being in Florida. Bennett being with her. She wasn't alone.

"So," Bennett started. "How about you give me a little more about my name."

She laughed having forgotten about the whole thing. "Receptive."

Bennett looked up thoughtfully, his fingers stroking his chin in mock-consideration. "Benevolent. Receptive. What about the 'W'?"

Caroline tip-toed to kiss him on the cheek. He blushed scarlet and Caroline loved every second of it. "You'll get that tomorrow."

They walked around campus aimlessly after that, talking about things that didn't have much weight. Caroline thought that they both understood that it wasn't the time to get into things that mattered. So, they just talked about simple things. Like favorite colors. Bennett's was blue. And ice cream flavors. He liked strawberry the most. Then they talked about whether or not they liked cats or dogs better. Bennett liked dogs more because cats were too sassy.

She wasn't sure how many times they had passed the Landis Green before it started getting dark. It was as if time hadn't existed in those moments. The only way they were able to tell that it was passing was by looking at the sky.

Bennett and Caroline eventually got back to the hotel, going up to their room hand-in-hand. After staying up so late the night before, Caroline was exhausted. She showered first again and got in bed, tucking herself into the covers and closing her eyes.

She saw her mother in front of her. She was beautiful, timeless. She sat on the Landis Green, smiling. The wind was rustling around them. Caroline felt cold, but her mother had warmth radiating from her skin. She was alive. Breathing. Until one moment, she just... wasn't. Her mother was wrapping her hands around her own neck. She was choking. Caroline was choking. She started turning blue. Caroline did as well. Caroline watched as her mother opened her mouth in a silent scream. The Landis Green disappeared around them, turning into darkness. Caroline tried to scream, but hers was silent as well.

"Caroline," her mother said.

Caroline began to sob. "Mom."

"*Caroline.*"

She opened her eyes. Bennett was shaking her softly. She felt the tears drying on her cheeks. She was crying just as she had been crying in her dream.

"Are you okay?" Bennett asked.

"Y-yeah," Caroline stuttered, still dazed. "I'm fine."

"You were crying," he said.

"I know," she said quietly.

"Are you sure you're okay?" he asked again.

Caroline didn't feel the nerves rising in her chest like she normally did after those dreams. She just felt... sad. She nodded, letting him know that she'd be fine, but as soon as he got up and turned away from her, she knew she needed him.

"Bennett?" she said quickly.

"Yeah?" he said as he turned back to face her.

"Can I get in bed with you?"

Bennett looked at her and nodded, reaching down to grab her hand. She got in bed with him and easily fit her back up again his stomach. He felt warm and comforted

and safe. He felt like the home she had been missing since her mother died. It was that feeling of safety that made her start talking.

"My mother had asked me to stay home the night she died. It was my birthday and I had already made plans with Izzy. I didn't think anything of it when I told her no. I thought I'd see her when I got home. I thought—" Caroline got choked up and had to swallow the lump in her throat. She knew she had told Bennett part of this story before, but it still hurt. This time, though, she had to tell him everything. "I thought she'd always be there."

Bennett waited patiently for her to continue her story even throughout all of the pauses and sniffles.

"When I got home that night," Caroline started again, "the lights were all off. Candles were burnt all the way down. It was too quiet even though it was late. I *knew* something was wrong. That's when I found her." Caroline stifled a sob. It was easier talking to Bennett when he wasn't looking at her. It felt like she was simply talking into the air with the whole world listening but no one hearing a word she said.

"She was holding her throat," she continued. "I tried to pry her hands away from herself, and then eventually gave up because her arms were locked in place. I started CPR, but she was already blue when I had first gotten home."

The room was quiet after that. All Caroline heard was the whirr of the AC.

"They think it was the antibiotics. They think she had an allergic reaction and died because her throat was too swollen for her to breathe. They said it could have taken anywhere from five to *fifteen* minutes. She could've been suffocating for fifteen minutes." She started crying then because it was what she was about to say that had hurt her the most after those past seven months. It was what kept hurting her still. "She wanted me to stay, Bennett. I could've... Maybe she wouldn't have—" Caroline started sobbing. Full body-shaking sobs that consumed her. "I could have saved her if I would have just stayed home."

Bennett wrapped his arms tightly around her, pulling her even closer to him. She felt warm against him, but so *so* cold everywhere else.

"You don't know what would've happened. She might have still died, but you'll just never know, Caro. That's the worst part—the not knowing—but you just can't know these things. So, you can't blame it on yourself."

"I wish it had been me, Bennett," Caroline sobbed. "I wish I would've died instead."

Bennett made her turn to face him even though she didn't want to. "You don't wish that, Caro. Your mother wouldn't have wished that. Izzy wouldn't have. Your grandparents wouldn't have. You *cannot* just give up."

"It hurts so much," she cried, trying to suck in air. She reached over abruptly and tried to get him to kiss her. It was a horrible thing to do in that situation—she knew that—but she just wanted that horrible empty feeling to *go away*.

Fix it.

"No, Caroline," Bennett said as he tried to stop her. "Caroline, *no*." He sat up and scooted away from her a bit. "I can't—"

"Bennett, please," she said.

"I can't be your crutch, Caroline," he said, his eyes wild and scared.

Caroline sat up and looked at him. He looked terrified. "Bennett, I—" she said, wanting to apologize as the tears still streamed down her face.

"No," Bennett said, sounding emotional. "I was—Josh made me—" Bennett tried to breathe just like Caroline was always trying to do. "I can't be your crutch," he said again, "because that's who I was to

Josh. I was his crutch. I let him forget and pretend and ignore it as much as he wanted, but it only made it worse for him. He fell deeper and deeper until I couldn't pull him out. He was depressed, Caroline, and I basically told him that it was okay to ignore it by letting him use me to forget. He took me to play baseball with him. He took me hiking. He asked me about you because he knew that I liked you. I lied to our parents because he asked me to. I told them that he was fine because *he asked me to*. He *used* me to forget so that he wouldn't have to face what was really wrong with him."

"Bennett, I'm sorry. I didn't realize—"

"No, you didn't," he said. "Don't make me be someone who helps you forget. Caroline, I—I really like you. But I can't be that person for you. I can't let you destroy yourself."

Caroline searched his eyes. He was hurt so much more than she could have ever imagined. "Okay," she said. "Okay, I'm sorry." She pulled him into a hug. "I'm so so sorry, Bennett." She buried her face in his chest and felt as his face buried into her hair.

She wasn't sure how long they stayed like that. She just knew that she had to make him feel better. "For the record," she whispered into his chest. "I really like you, too." Caroline felt as he held her tighter, refusing to let her go. "Now we both know each other's secrets," Caroline said.

Bennett pulled away from her a bit. "Not all of my secrets," he said as he looked down at her. "Do you remember when I said that Josh wanted to be a lawyer?"

Caroline nodded. She had been wondering about it since they had talked about it at the airport.

"I went into it because that's what my dad wanted me to do. I guess that's what he wanted Josh to do, too, but he basically told me that since Josh couldn't become a lawyer, I had to."

"You didn't have to listen to him, Bennett."

Bennett got choked up as he tried to speak again. "I did, though," he finally said. "Josh was… Josh was his golden child. The son he always wanted. When he died, my dad just—" Bennett shut his eyes tightly and grimaced. "He wanted me to be Josh. So, I started doing everything that Josh used to do with my dad. My mom was too busy with her grief to even notice. They've both even called me Josh before," Bennett said as his voice cracked. "Sometimes—"

He stopped talking and Caroline knew what he was feeling. The choking feeling. The feeling as if the darkness would take everything and there'd be nothing left. She reached for his hand and squeezed, urging him to continue.

"Sometimes it feels like I died instead of him. Sometimes, they make me feel like that. Like Bennett is the one who is gone. I just—" He shook his head. "I just wanted to make them feel better. That's why I never said no."

Caroline scooted over to him to where they were both sitting cross-legged with their knees touching as they faced each other. She reached out and held his face, searching his eyes. "We keep going," she said because it was the only thing that she could think to say in a time like that.

Bennett smiled and nodded as he wiped a single tear from his face. "You and me."

She crawled into his lap and wrapped her arms and legs around him, holding him close. "I'm sorry,

Bennett," she said again. "I won't use you to forget. You won't be my crutch."

"Use me to remember, Caro. I want us to remember everything."

She nuzzled her head into the crook between his shoulder and his neck. "Benevolent Bennett. Receptive. Winsome."

He pulled back quickly. "Winsome?" There was humor alight in his features. "*Winsome*?"

"What?" Caroline laughed.

"What does that even mean?"

They both started laughing as they fell back against the bed side-by-side. It felt good to laugh with him. Even if she still wouldn't go to FSU. Even if she couldn't tell him that until college was about to start and there would be no turning back. She just laughed because there seemed to be no other way for her to go on. She couldn't be in Florida alone. Bennett just didn't understand that.

"It means," she said as she caught her breath. "That you have an amazing personality."

"Good or bad thing?" he asked, holding back another laugh.

"One hundred percent good," she giggled. "You've got everything: the personality, the looks, the intelligence."

"Funny," Bennett said. "Everyone always called me nerdy."

Caroline raised her eyebrows mischievously and tilted her head up. "Who ever said that being nerdy was a *bad* thing?"

As if on cue, Bennett pushed his glasses up the bridge of his nose and Caroline couldn't stop herself from smiling. He was adorable, and she was so grateful that they found their way back to each other. She prayed and hoped that he wouldn't hate her after she stayed in Arizona. Even though she wanted nothing more than to be able to attend FSU. Even though by staying in Arizona, she was doing the one thing that he begged her not to do: using him to forget.

Chapter 19

Caroline woke up with Bennett's arms wrapped tightly around her. She wasn't ready to get up, but her stomach growled in protest. Bennett was still fast asleep and she wondered how much longer he had stayed up after Caroline had dozed off.

She thought about what he had said last night. She thought about Josh asking him not to tell their parents. She thought about Josh doing so many things with Bennett to keep himself occupied. She knew what it felt like to try and drown out the thoughts coming from your own mind. It felt a lot like filling up your schedule so there wasn't an ounce of time left. She thought about how Bennett's parents had just wanted to forget. How, instead of remembering Josh, they had used Bennett to replace him. She thought about how Bennett begged her not to use him as a crutch. What other choice did she have, though? If she let her grandparents and Izzy and Bennett convince her that she could make it alone in Florida, she would wind up there and have no one to pick up the pieces when she broke. She would have the darkness following her everywhere. She wouldn't be able to escape. That kind of pain? That kind of darkness? Might just turn her to depression, and might just make her like Josh.

When she pulled gently away from Bennett, he stirred slightly but didn't wake. She got dressed and went downstairs to get breakfast. It was nine o'clock in the morning, so it was still early enough to where they hadn't started picking anything up at all.

Caroline went straight to the waffle-maker and made four of them before even attempting to get anything else. By the time she was done getting breakfast, though, she had ultimately had to get help from an attendant to bring everything back up to the room.

She thanked the man graciously and gave him a twenty-dollar bill for being so helpful. Bennett was just starting to wake up when the man left the room and Caroline began doctoring her waffles with syrup and fruit.

"You weren't going to wake me?" Bennett asked as he sat up groggily.

"I mean... I was.... Just after I finished eating all the waffles," Caroline said as she put another piece into her mouth. It tasted amazing even though it was just a plain old waffle with fruit and syrup. Caroline had to stop herself from closing her eyes in enjoyment to avoid looking completely idiotic.

Bennett shook his head as he smiled at her and came to sit next to her. "Do I get one of those?" he asked.

She looked up at him with the fork halfway to her mouth. "Maybe."

Caroline eventually relented and he got two of the four waffles. She had made way more food than either of them could eat, so she was barely able to finish them anyway.

"What's on the agenda for today?" Bennett asked.

"You? swimsuit. Us? Beach."

Bennett laughed and nearly spit out his coffee. "Okay, okay," he said.

So, after they finished their breakfast, they both got dressed and packed various items for the beach. Caroline—coming prepared—had a towel and bathing suit ready. She put her bathing suit on with clothes over it. She put her towel, sunscreen, and sunglasses into a beach bag, fully prepared for their outing.

"You make me look like a slacker," Bennett said as he looked at her ensemble.

Caroline shrugged. "We're in *Florida*, Bennett."

They shared a secret smile and left. They had to get a ride to the nearest beach store to find a swimsuit for Bennett. What made Caroline laugh, though, was the fact that all the men's swimsuits were extremely short. So, when Bennett came out wearing them and they stopped only a few inches below his waist, Caroline couldn't stop herself from snorting.

"I knew they looked ridiculous," Bennett said as he pushed his glasses up the bridge of his nose.

"No, no," Caroline wheezed, trying to catch her breath. "Those are totally in style right now." She eventually was able to stop herself from laughing, but she had to admit, the swimsuit was pretty cute on him.

So, they paid at the front and Bennett changed into his swimsuit. The nearest beach, though, was about an hour away, so the drive there was pretty boring. Bennett and Caroline just sat in the backseat of the ride they had called for. They held hands and whispered as if they had to be quiet.

"You don't have to answer, Caro," Bennett started as he drew circles on her hand with his pointer finger, "but I know you love it here. I know you said you wanted to stay in Arizona, but I think you're lying still—even to yourself." He was still whispering even though they both knew it wasn't necessary. "But I just wanted to let you know that this trip has made me sure of one thing: I won't be going back to Massachusetts. I don't even know if I'm going to go back to college at all."

"Bennett…" Caroline started as she looked up at him. "This is what you want?"

"Yes," he said.

"Then I'm happy for you. I really am." She laid her head on his chest as she said that. What she was thinking, though, on top of being happy for him, was that he'd stay in Arizona. With her. And somehow, that made the decision to not go to Florida even more solidified in her mind. They could be together. Just her and Bennett.

When they got to the beach, Caroline and Bennett set up all of their things in a quiet little corner. This beach was in a national park, so it was secluded enough to where there weren't many other people around. It also wasn't a beach that you'd typically see in a picture of a Florida beach. It had grassy patches near them and wasn't very large or full of "endless white sand." Almost everyone was sunbathing except for a few kids. Caroline wondered how they could resist the temptation of the water. She took off all of her clothes and made sure that her bathing suit was secure and in place. The sun felt good against Caroline's skin and she couldn't wait to get in the water.

"Together?" she asked Bennett as she grabbed his hand and looked out to the water.

He pulled his shirt off over his head and smiled at her. "Together."

They ran out into the water and not more than four steps in, hit a drop off and sunk below the surface. The cold hit Caroline like a million little daggers. She popped her head above the water and gasped for breath. She saw Bennett surface beside her.

"O-oh my g-g-gosh," she said, her teeth chattering. "It's f-freezing." She started as she swam back to where she could stand and climbed out of the water. How could the sun feel so warm and the water feel so *not*?

"B-b-but," Bennett started as he tried to get out of the water and ended up under the surface a few more times. "I-it's *F-F-Florida*." He climbed out of the water next to where Caroline was standing and stood up.

Caroline glared at him with her arms wrapped around herself. She reached out and pushed him back into the water, running swiftly away to the safety of their towels. She shook as she wrapped the towel around herself and pulled out her stupid list.

Things to do with Bennett in Florida:

1. ~~Tour campus :(~~

2. ~~Go to the Sweet Shop (where Mom and Dad met).~~

3. ~~Picnic at Landis Green.~~

4. ~~Go to the beach (because we're in Florida and it's a must).~~

She basically scratched out all the letters to the "Go to the beach" part to where it was almost at the point of being illegible. The napkin was a shredded mess by that point. How was the water that cold? In March? In *Florida*?

"That was rude," Bennett said as he came to sit down beside her, grabbing his towel and wrapping it around himself.

Caroline scooted next to him despite the fact that she was still peeved by his comment. "You basically made me do it."

Bennett laughed and Caroline bumped him with her shoulder.

"Why is it even that cold in the water?" Caroline complained. "It isn't that cold out here."

Bennett shrugged. "I guess we should've seen it coming. The water doesn't heat up as fast as the temperature out here does."

She assumed he was right, but it still made her annoyed.

Together, they ended up like most of the other people out there: sunbathing. Caroline could feel her skin baking, but it felt so good to feel warmth going all the way through her even if it was uncomfortable at times. The heat made her sleepy, so she looked over at Bennett.

"Mind if I take a nap?" she asked.

"Hmm?" he mumbled, already sounding asleep.

Caroline smiled as she flipped over onto her stomach and closed her eyes again, feeling so beautifully at peace.

When Caroline's eyes fluttered open sometime later, she felt as if she was still sleeping. Her skin felt raw from staying in the sun for so long and it hurt to move too much. She was groggy and disoriented. When she rolled over to reach for Bennett—with dread filling her stomach—she realized that she was alone.

Caroline jolted up and felt completely awake. She winced as her sunburnt skin moved. She looked around and the beach was completely empty. She was the only one there. Even Bennett's things were gone.

Breathe.

She was going to throw up. She was definitely going to throw up. Caroline became hyperaware of everything. Her fingers and toes began to tingle. She had to clear her throat because it felt scratchy and dry. Her lungs began to heave with the effort it took to take a breath.

You're alone.

One. Two.

You're going to die.

One. Two.

Just breathe.

One.

Fix it.

"Bennett?" Caroline called as she stood up. Her legs were shaky and unstable. She started to hyperventilate. Everything felt so cold. Caroline turned in a complete circle, not a soul in sight. "*Bennett!*" she screamed, falling to her knees and wrapping herself up in a ball. She tucked her head into her knees and began hysterically sobbing.

You're alone.

"Caroline? Caro?" Someone was shaking her. "Caroline, look at me."

Her head was pried away from her knees as she looked through her tears at the person in front of her.

"Bennett?" she squeaked, relief beginning to wash over her. Relief but then unimaginable anger. "Where *were* you?" she cried as she shoved him away.

"I called a ride for us. I went to go put our bags in the car. I was gone only a few minutes, Caro. You were asleep." He looked frantic and concerned. Bennett reached for her, but she pulled away.

"I was alone," she cried as she stood up. He stood up with her.

"Caroline, I swear I was going to come right back. I didn't want to wake you up until we had to leave. You just—you looked so peaceful."

Rationally, she knew she shouldn't be mad, but she had been so scared. She had been terrified. She had been alone, and she knew that she could never be alone. He had left her alone.

"You just don't understand," she yelled at him. "I can't—I can't be alone."

"Caro," he said as he reached out to touch her shoulder. She flinched. "Caro, we keep going remember? You can make it through this. You can still go to FSU, and you will be fine because *we keep going.*"

"Just you and me, right?" she laughed harshly. "You won't be here, Bennett. No one will be here."

"I know you, Caroline. You are strong and brave and I know that—"

"You're not listening to me!" she nearly screamed. Caroline's skin was prickling, and she knew she should stop herself but she just couldn't keep the words from spilling out of her. "I'm not going to FSU, Bennett. I'm never going to go to FSU."

He looked stunned and hurt and disappointed all at once.

She softened her tone a little as she reached out to him. "I'm going to stay in Arizona with my grandparents. With *you*. We can be together." She smiled at him, but his frown deepened.

"You were never even going to consider coming to Florida, were you?" he asked, looking hurt and betrayed.

She scoffed. "I mean, look at me, Bennett. I'd never make it out here by myself."

He shook his head as he took a step away from her. "You're just holding yourself back," he said. "I'm not going to let you use me as an excuse to stay in Arizona."

"Bennett, no," she said, closing the distance between them. "No, you said you wanted to stay. I was going to stay anyway. I was—"

"That's not the point, Caroline!" he yelled.

She nearly jumped back. She had never heard him yell before. He was always quiet and kind and sweet and understanding.

"You are going to stay in Arizona instead of trying to help yourself. You're just going to push everything and everyone away until you don't have to worry about your own feelings. You're just going to keep trying to forget rather than trying to actually *fix it*."

Those words felt like a slap to the face to Caroline. Hadn't she been trying to fix it? Wasn't staying in Arizona helping her fix it?

"Bennett," she said as she grabbed his hand.

He pulled it away roughly. "No. Caroline…. Just—" He grimaced and shook his head. "I can't be here for you. I can't be that person. I'm just starting to see that I need to be my own person. I'm just starting to understand how to heal. I can't help you drown when I'm trying so hard to stay afloat."

"Are you…" Caroline started slowly, feeling her stomach drop. "You don't want to be with me?"

"I *can't* be with you," he cringed. "I want to be with you, Caro. I've always wanted that. But you and me, we just—we aren't okay. We have to be okay by ourselves before we can ever be okay together."

"Bennett, please," she begged.

"Let's go home, Caroline." He sounded defeated. He sounded tired.

Caroline felt the tears falling down her cheeks. It couldn't be real. The whole past hour had to just be some sick nightmare that she wasn't waking up from.

Bennett was walking away from her in the direction of where Caroline assumed the car was waiting. She looked down at her feet when he got out of her eyesight. She watched as her tears hit the sand and didn't even bother to wipe them away. She slipped on her clothes and felt the list of things to do with Bennett in her pocket. She pulled it out and ripped what was left of the napkin into tiny pieces. There was only one part that she didn't rip:

6. Don't think.

Chapter 20

That night had been excruciating. Caroline had showered and gotten in bed. Bennett had told her that he was going downstairs. That he'd just be a text away if she needed him. Then he left. He hadn't come back, and when Caroline had woken up the next morning, he already had everything packed.

Caroline had quickly thrown on her clothes that she had picked out for the flight home. She had packed her things and followed Bennett downstairs into the lobby of the hotel. The hotel provided them a shuttle bus, so they didn't have to call a ride, but Caroline couldn't even remember the last time she had been that quiet around Bennett. Or anyone for that matter. They weren't talking to each other, and it really hurt Caroline. The thing that hurt the most, though, was how sad Bennett looked. He had no more anger etched into his features. Just exhaustion and a whole lot of sadness.

When they eventually boarded their flight back to Arizona, Caroline felt as if it would be a good time to try to get him to talk to her.

"Bennett, can we talk please?" She reached for his hand. Thankfully, there was no one in the seat beside them.

He gently pulled his hand away and Caroline had never known before that moment that it was possible to push someone away gently.

"Please, Bennett," Caroline said, the pleading in her voice evident.

"What is there to talk about, Caroline?" he asked tiredly. "I've told you everything. I told you how I feel. I told you about my brother and how he leaned on me and made sure that our parents never found out about him. I told you how much I didn't want to be used to forget your problems. You still did it, though."

Caroline let her head hang. She felt ashamed but wasn't sure what else she was supposed to do. She couldn't go to Florida. So, staying in Arizona with Bennett just seemed logical. She knew that he would feel hurt when he found out about her actually wanting to go to Florida, but she hadn't realized just how bad it would be.

"Is there anything I can do to make this better?" she asked desperately.

"You have to try."

"Try what?" Caroline asked, feeling hope fluttering in her chest.

"You have to try to get better."

She wasn't sure what to say to that. She had been trying so hard to stay afloat just like he said he was trying to do. Didn't he get that? Didn't he understand how hard she was trying?

They didn't talk for the rest of the trip. The plane landed a few hours later, they got their bags, and left the airport. He drove her home and barely said a word as Caroline removed her bags from his car.

She went up to the driver's side window in one last desperate attempt to make him change his mind. "Bennett, I don't want it to end like this."

He looked over at her and reached out to hold her face. "This doesn't have to be the end, Caro. You get to make that decision." He pulled her down and kissed her cheek. Then, he drove away.

Caroline wanted to start crying again. She wanted to get in her car and drive. She wanted to erase the last few weeks. But the problem was, she couldn't do that no matter how much she wanted to. So, she grabbed her things and walked to the front door.

When she finally decided to open the door, she noticed that Izzy's car was in the driveway and her Grams' car was missing. Caroline unlocked the front door and walked in, hoping that it wasn't another ambush like when they found out about her acceptance letters.

Inside, she found Izzy fidgeting on the couch. Her grams and gramps were nowhere to be found.

"Izzy?" Caroline said.

Izzy nearly fell over. When she looked over at Caroline, she smiled nervously and stood up. "Caroline!" she said, way overenthusiastically. "How was your trip?"

"Izzy," Caroline said slowly. "Where are Grams and Gramps?"

"They just…." Izzy trailed off. "They're just…."

"Izzy?" Caroline raised her eyebrows and tried to get Izzy to look at her.

"They didn't want you to worry—"

"Izzy, where are they?" Caroline asked, more nervously.

"They're at the hospital…." Izzy said. "But don't freak out, they don't want you to worry or anything."

"*Izzy*," Caroline said frantically, her stomach dropping within her. She felt as if her heart was skipping beats. "Why are they at the hospital?"

Izzy looked down at her feet. "They think Gramps had a heart attack."

"*What?*" Caroline squeaked. "Wha—When did this happen?"

"Earlier this morning. But they really don't want you to get worried or anything—"

"I'm sure they don't," Caroline said as she interrupted Izzy. She felt tears prickling behind her eyes. They didn't want her to know about it because they were worried that she'd break. They had wanted to hide it from her because they didn't think she could handle it. *Gramps* was in the hospital. Her knees felt like they were going to give way. Her fingertips began having the familiar sensation of tingling in them. "A heart attack?" Caroline asked.

Izzy nodded.

Caroline's stomach dropped again and she felt on the verge of something big. Something very *very* dark. "Please," Caroline whispered. "Please, take me there." She tried to keep herself calm, but she was finding it very hard.

"I don't think that's a good idea," Izzy said quietly as she touched Caroline's arm.

"I'm so tired of everyone tip-toeing around me, Iz. It's the whole reason that I didn't want people to know. I—" she started but began to feel choked up midway. "The only person who didn't act like I was going to break was Bennett, but now he's—"

"Caro," Izzy said, looking concerned. "What happened?"

"I messed it up, Izzy. I screwed everything up just like I always do." Caroline started crying then and could barely see Izzy through her tears. Too much was happening. Too much was spinning and changing around her. She felt like she was going to fall.

Izzy grabbed her arm to steady her, and then looked into her eyes. "Let's go," Izzy said as she reached for Caroline's hand.

Caroline took Izzy's hand and held it as she walked her to her car outside. Izzy drove them to the hospital and held Caroline's hand the whole entire time, even when they got to the front desk to ask what room her gramps was in.

Caroline felt numb. She felt out of control. She felt so distant from herself that she could hardly make her feet move. But she was moving. She had to remember that. She and Izzy were moving, and Caroline had to keep going. *We keep going.* The mantra made her want to cry, but she stayed strong.

When they got up to the room and stood outside, Izzy took Caroline by the shoulders and looked into her eyes. "Caroline, whatever happens in there—no matter how sick Gramps is—none of us think you're broken," Izzy said as she also started to get choked up with tears. Caroline still hadn't stopped crying. "I've never thought you were broken, Caro. You're so strong and resilient and brave. You've been dealing with this basically on your own and I feel so bad that I didn't know—" she squeaked. "You're not broken. You're just a little lost, that's all. Okay?"

Caroline nodded as she felt her throat constrict. She wanted to say something to Izzy. She wanted to tell her that she's the best friend Caroline had ever had. She wanted to tell Izzy that she had been there even if she didn't know what was going on. But she couldn't say anything. She just kept nodding and nodding until a sob escaped her throat and Izzy pulled her into a hug.

"I love you, Caro," Izzy cried.

"I love you too," Caroline whispered into her friend's shoulder.

Then, they composed themselves and tried to look as brave as possible as they knocked on the door and walked into her gramps' hospital room.

The beeping of so many machines scared Caroline at first, but she realized that the rhythmic beeping was actually a good thing. It meant that Gramps was still alive and okay.

Grams was sitting in a chair beside Gramps' bed, her head in her hands. She looked tired and scared.

"Grams?" Caroline said quietly. It seemed as if her Gramps was sleeping.

Her grams looked up and tears filled her eyes. "Oh, Caroline," Grams said as she stood to embrace her. Grams wrapped her in a huge hug and Caroline felt the tears coming again.

"Is he—?" Caroline started, but the tears stopped her. "Is he gonna be okay?"

Grams nodded vigorously through her tears. "It was just a small heart attack. He had a blockage that they went in to fix. He'll be fine, Caroline."

Relief flooded Caroline as she nearly fell to the floor. "Oh," she gasped as her voice distorted from her emotions. "Oh, thank God," she cried, finally feeling like she could let her guard down.

Grams wrapped her in another hug. "He scared us all, didn't he?"

Caroline nodded.

"He wants to talk to you, Caroline. He has something for you."

Caroline looked at her Grams questioningly, and then over at her gramps. He was smiling weakly at her.

"Did you think I'd leave you, kiddo?"

She basically ran over to him and wrapped her arms around him. She vaguely processed the fact that her grams and Izzy left the room. "You can't do that again. You're not allowed," Caroline cried into his chest.

He petted her hair. "Your grams nearly killed me for this, too," he chuckled. "But like I told you, kiddo, I'm as healthy as a horse."

Caroline sat down in the chair that her grams was in and took Gramps' hand.

"How was Florida?" he asked, hope glimmering in his eyes.

"First of all," Caroline started, pointing her finger at him, "I cannot *believe* you stuffed those condoms in my bag, Gramps!"

Her gramps blushed furiously but laughed all the same. "Your grams would've had my head if she found out you left them behind. I had to."

She shook her head, and they began laughing together. Then, Caroline felt the events of the weekend hit her all at once, making the laughter stop.

"Gramps, I—" Caroline said getting choked up. "I can't go to Florida."

"Why not, kiddo? I can already tell that you loved it there." His wrinkles intensified as he gave her a warm smile. He seemed weaker than normal, but still the same plucky old man that she had always known.

"I can't be there alone, Gramps. I mean—" she stopped herself. "What if this happens again? What if you or Grams get sick? I can't leave you guys. I can't—I just can't be alone."

"Your grams and I will be fine. Even if we get sick, you can still get a flight back with no problems. Kiddo," he said as he grabbed her hand with both of his own cold ones, "you can't stop living life even when the people you love most leave you."

"Gramps, you don't understand," Caroline cried. She was finally going to tell him. "She asked me to stay the night she died. She wanted me to stay home with her. Maybe if I—If I would have stayed, she'd— It's all my fault," Caroline sobbed, pulling her hand away from her gramps to hide her face.

But he held on tight and fiercely as he said her name. "None of this was your fault. Don't you ever say that again. Your mother died and it was because of something that no one could've controlled or changed. Did you know she got the antibiotics from me? I gave her that prescription, Caroline, but that doesn't mean that it's my fault. And you not staying in that night? That doesn't make it your fault the same way that giving her the medicine doesn't make it mine." Gramps had tears in his eyes as he held her hand tightly. "I loved your mother so much. She was my little girl. Your grams and I, we tried so hard to make sure that you got everything you needed after she died, and I think we missed the most important thing."

Caroline wiped the tears from the corners of her eyes. "What?"

"We forgot to tell you that it's okay to feel broken. It's okay to hurt and to feel pain and to *grieve*. Everything that you have felt is *okay* to feel, and I am so sorry, Caroline, that we never made that clearer to you. This whole time we should have been letting you feel everything because you cannot understand and process those feelings unless you are actually allowed to feel them."

Gramps was crying with Caroline when he finished talking, and Caroline couldn't imagine that he didn't hate her after what she had told him. She thought that he'd blame her. She thought so many things. She just wished that she could get rid of the darkness.

"I have something for you," Gramps said as they pulled away from each other. "We were cleaning out your mother's house this weekend and I found a birthday present."

Caroline's heart began beating wildly in her chest. Her birthday present? The last gift that her mother had for her. The one Caroline had desperately wished to see.

Gramps pulled a small box from his bedside table. It was wrapped in brown paper wrapping with a small blue ribbon tied into a bow on top. "It's for you, Caroline," he said as he handed her the small box.

Caroline's hands shook as she slowly undid the ribbon. She opened the brown wrapping paper slowly and found a velvet box underneath it. When she opened the box, a small locket lay inside. It was oval and looked antique. When Caroline went to open the locket, a small folded up piece of paper fell out. It was a note of some sort and Caroline felt her lungs constrict as she unfolded the paper. What she saw, though, made a sob escape her throat. Because what she saw? It changed everything.

Chapter 21

11 Years Earlier

When Caroline came home that day, she knew something was off. She couldn't pinpoint what was wrong exactly except that she knew there was something that wasn't right. There was something about the air that didn't feel right. The house was too quiet. She couldn't smell supper cooking on the stovetop. Even though she was only seven (and a half), she understood that things were not normal. That's why when she found her mother breathing fast, curled into a ball on the recliner, her head buried in her knees, Caroline understood what was wrong. Her mother was sleeping this time, clutching a picture of Caroline's father. It looked like she was having a very *very* bad dream. Sometimes, these things happened often. Sometimes, they didn't happen at all.

It had started after her father died. She wasn't exactly sure where people went when they "died" except that it meant her dad wasn't ever coming home. Because of this, Caroline's mother disappeared sometimes. Not like hide-and-seek disappear… just kind of like peek-a-boo where people pretended to be gone but were only hiding behind their hands. Somehow, Caroline often had to show her mom how to pull her hands back from her face. Sometimes it was with Izzy's help. Sometimes, Caroline called her grandparents by using her mother's forgotten cell phone. Sometimes, Caroline just had to figure it out by herself.

"Can I talk to Izzy, please?" Caroline said, holding the cell phone with two hands just like her mother taught her.

"Of course, Caroline, give me one second," Izzy's mother said. Izzy's mother always seemed so put together, so perfectly whole. At least, that's what Caroline thought.

"Hey, Caroline!" Izzy sang.

Caroline smiled, appreciating Izzy's bubbly personality, wanting to make it her own. She wanted to ask Izzy to come over. She wanted to ask Izzy about Maxwell—Izzy's puppy—or about the twinkling lights that her parents bought for her room, or even about school. "It's happening again," Caroline said instead.

Caroline could feel Izzy getting very serious on the other end of the phone. "I can't come over today, Caroline," she said, her voice losing the cheery tone.

"What should I do?" Caroline asked.

Izzy was quiet for a few moments. "When my mom gets upset, she always likes to light candles and put on her favorite music. Sometimes she even bakes cookies. Just whatever makes her happy, I guess. You could maybe make her some hot chocolate, too."

Caroline thought about this and nodded even though Izzy couldn't see her. After a few seconds of silence, Caroline remembered to reply. "Yeah, that does sound good."

After this, Caroline hung up the phone. While she microwaved the milk, she rummaged around in the pantry to find the hot cocoa mix. Once she heard the *ding*, she got the powder, poured it into the mug with the milk, and began to stir. The warm mug felt good in her hands as she walked across the cold, tiled floor in the kitchen. Once she reached the living room, she placed the hot cocoa near her mother and grabbed the TV remote. She searched for the music app and once she found it, put it on her mother's favorite station. The deep, low, melodic singing began echoing throughout the house.

Caroline walked over to a few of the windows and opened up the curtains. She knew how much her mother loved the light and the cool air, so she opened up a few windows as well. As the breeze wafted into the house, Caroline shivered, goosebumps crawling up her arms and legs. She ran down the hallway into her mother's room.

Her mother's huge sweater was laying discarded on the bed. Caroline grabbed it, feeling its warmth on her fingertips. She ran back down the hallway but stopped and turned around. She grabbed her own fuzzy sweater out of her room and slipped it on, shivering once more as warmth circulated through her body.

When she got back into the living room, her mother was no longer on the recliner. The hot chocolate was gone, too.

"What do you think you're doing?"

Caroline whipped around to see her mother standing in the kitchen, hot cocoa raised to her strawberry lips. She could smell the chocolatey drink as her mother sipped it.

"I wanted to make you happy," Caroline said matter-of-factly.

Caroline's mother shook her head and smiled sadly. "Come here, Sunshine Caroline." She opened her arms widely and let Caroline slip the sweater onto her mother's arms. Her mother then raised Caroline up into her arms and held her tight. "You make me happy," she said.

"Izzy said that if I did a few of your favorite things that it would make you feel better," Caroline mumbled into her mother's neck.

Her mother pulled her away from her chest and put her down. "Oh, she did, did she?" Her mother looked amused as she raised her eyebrow. It made Caroline feel warm inside. "What else was on your list of things to do?"

Caroline held out her hand and began counting on her fingers. "I was going to light candles, and I was going to make cookies, but that one is a little hard."

Her mother laughed. It was a beautiful, melodious sound. One that Caroline didn't hear nearly enough. "Okay, well I think we can take care of that together."

Then, Caroline and her mother went around the house, lighting every candle they could find. They even took some out of storage. There were small candles that Caroline could fit in the palm of her hand and big candles that she could barely hold. They put them out all over the kitchen and living room and lit every single one. It was a weird mix of smells. Caroline smelled pine needles and cinnamon and apples and pumpkin and cranberries and every smell that made cold weather even better.

As her mother went to preheat the oven, she then walked around and turned out all the lights. Caroline nearly gasped. The whole room glowed with the light from the candles and the sunset coming through the windows. This was better than the twinkling lights in Izzy's room. This was better than Christmas and better than Thanksgiving and even better than Halloween when there was more candy than Caroline could possibly eat. What made it better than all of those things, though, wasn't the candles, the smells, the cold air, or even the warmth coming from the oven. It was the smile on her mother's face, lit up not only by the candles, but by the happiness that Caroline thought was the best thing in the world. She ran to her mother and hugged her fiercely, refusing to let go.

"I love you," she whispered.

"I love you too, my sweet Sunshine Caroline."

Together, they started making chocolate chip cookies. The house was the perfect temperature in between cool and warm. Her mother poured ingredients and Caroline stirred. The music got changed to Christmas songs even though it was nowhere near close to Christmastime. They sang about Rudolph, sleigh rides, silent nights (even though there was nothing silent about this one), wanting only each other for Christmas, Frosty, and being home for Christmas. The room began to smell something like chocolate-cranberry-pine-cinnamon-apple cookies, and it felt like before to Caroline.

Before her father had died. Before her mother got sad. Before the house felt so wrong.

The cookies came out of the oven and the house fell silent. The TV read, "Are you still listening?" and the Christmas music stopped playing. Caroline's mother made two more mugs of hot chocolate, giving one to Caroline and keeping one for herself. They ate their cookies in relative silence, sipping on the hot cocoa, the chocolate cookies melting in their mouths. Caroline thought about how she hadn't had supper yet, but it didn't matter. Nothing mattered but her mother being happy again. She thought about everything she had done to make her mother happy.

"What're you thinking about over there?" her mother asked.

"I'm just thinking about all the little things that make you happy," Caroline said as she took another bite of her third cookie.

Her mother smiled, the light flickering across her face, but the light went away with the sun, and the warmth turned to coldness. Caroline shivered. Her mother closed the windows. She went to blow out the candles, but Caroline couldn't bear for the night to be over.

"Not yet," she pleaded.

Her mother nodded.

Caroline looked over to the refrigerator, reading the "Remember" list hanging there. Remember: milk. Remember: eggs. Remember: bills. Remember: dad's birthday.

Her mother followed Caroline's gaze to the fridge. Caroline watched as her mother took down the "Remember" list, ripping the top list away. The "Remember" was blank now.

"How about this?" her mother started, the smile growing on her face. "How about we list the things that make us happy, so we never forget? And every time we start to get sad, we have to add to our list of things." Caroline's mother was rustling through drawers, taking out colorful pens and pencils.

Caroline had never thought of a better idea than the one her mother just had. This would be it. This would be the way to keep her mother from hiding behind her hands.

In beautiful, scrawly script and Caroline's adolescent handwriting, they wrote:

Caroline and Elizabeth's Happiness List of All the Little Things

"Cold weather," her mother started. She wrote this under the title of the list.

"Cookies," Caroline added.

"Florida State University," her mother smiled. The place where her mother and father met.

"Hugs," Caroline said as she looked up at her mother in admiration.

"Hugs," her mother agreed.

It went like this for some time. Caroline and her mother went back and forth between the things that made them happy. They both agreed that only the most important things could be put on the first list. So, each item had to be especially important. There were things that made them smile, and some things that made their smiles sad, but they never stopped smiling.

When they were done, her mother pulled the list from the stack and put it on the fridge with a magnet. Caroline stared up at it and smiled as she reached for her mother's hand.

Remember
<u>Caroline and Elizabeth's Happiness List of All the Little</u>
<u>Things</u>

1. Cold weather
2. Cookies
3. Florida State University
4. Hugs
5. Gramps and Grams
6. Each other
7. Izzy
8. Our house
9. Christmas music
10. Daddy

As her mother got tired and Caroline followed her to bed, Caroline wondered about the list and how it would keep happiness in their house. She laid in the bed with her mother, staring up at the ceiling, and listening as her mother slowly fell asleep. Caroline wasn't sure how long she stayed awake, but she eventually got out of bed. She looked over to her mother and pulled the sheets close to her mother's face.

Caroline got into the living room and looked at the pictures of her little family lining the walls. Her father held her on his shoulders when they went to the water park. Her mother looked up at them both with so much love in her eyes. There was another picture of Caroline sitting cross-legged across from her mother, their heads leaning up against each other, smiling goofily, and looking into each other's eyes. The last picture Caroline looked at was of her mother and father. They looked like they were right in the middle of a conversation. Some secret that no one else knew. What made Caroline stop, though— something she had never noticed before—was the look in her father's eyes. It was the look that her mother gave her tonight. A look that her mother and father shared. A look of so much love that it made Caroline's heart start beating loudly in her chest. It was the smile and the love and the laughter that Caroline had been missing.

She walked over to the fridge and stared at the list. She thought about the cookies and the cold weather and the Christmas music. She thought about their house. She thought about hugs and having each other. She thought about her Grams and Gramps. She thought about Izzy. She thought about Florida State University and how her parents met there. She thought about how happy it would make her mother if she went there. She thought about her father. All of those little things made Caroline and her mother happy. All of those little things kept them together and kept them whole. She thought about those things all night.

For a long time, the list kept them whole. It kept them happy and laughing and together. Caroline didn't have to pull her mother's hands away from her face anymore. She didn't have to call Izzy or her grandparents for advice on how to help her mother. For a long time, the list gave them hope and kept them encouraged. After all, Caroline's father was on that list, and he wouldn't want them to be hiding. Even though he was gone, he was still a reason for their happiness. For a long time, the list was enough. Her father's memory was enough.

Caroline and her mother fell into a routine. The list fell from the magnet, floated down, and got lost under the fridge. It was forgotten, but their happiness was not. They planned Caroline's future. They talked about her going to FSU, to the place where her mother and father met. They baked cookies and felt the cool air and lit candles and listened to Christmas music and hugged each other more times than Caroline could count. It was a happiness that was immeasurable and boundless. It was a happiness that did not disappear even after the list was gone.

One day while cleaning the kitchen, her mother found the list behind the fridge. She looked at her daughter's childlike handwriting and her own script, seeing the beauty in both. It was a list that had saved her from her darkest moments, and she somehow knew that one day it would have to save Caroline. She couldn't say how she knew, but she felt it so strongly that she could not deny the purpose of the list. Her mother wrote one more line on the aging piece of paper and stashed it away. So, when she was gone and Caroline left an orphan, the list was there, tucked away, waiting to be found. It did not have big, life-altering information on it. It did not change the world. It did not take away the pain. It was a happiness list. It was a list of cookies, cold weather, Christmas music, a place that was like home, a place that was home, loved ones, and the ones who they never stopped loving—even after they were gone. It was a list of all the little things.

Remember

<u>Caroline and Elizabeth's Happiness List of All the Little Things</u>

1. Cold weather
2. Cookies
3. Florida State University
4. Hugs
5. Gramps and Grams
6. Each other
7. Izzy
8. Our house
9. Christmas music
10. Daddy
11. **The strength of my daughter**

Chapter 22

It was the list. The list of all the little things. The happiness list. The list that Caroline had forgotten existed. The list that changed both her and her mother's lives from that point on. Her mother had been depressed—that much was clear to Caroline now—but she kept going for Caroline. She kept trying and got better for *Caroline*.

Caroline wasn't stupid. Her mother hadn't magically gotten better after that list. She had moments where the depression came back. Caroline could remember those moments. But the list was magic to her. Just like FSU had been the magical kingdom, the list was the magical cure, and her mother had written that it was Caroline's strength that made her happy.

She gave the list to her gramps so that he could read it. She wasn't sure if he knew the story or not, but he cried just the same.

Her mother made her into the person she was. Caroline could feel more strength in that moment than she had ever felt. *It's what she would've wanted.* Her mother wanted her to go to FSU. Not because that was where she went, but because that was what Caroline had *always* wanted. It was time for Caroline to start facing her problems rather than hiding them behind her hands.

***

Dr. B and Caroline were sitting in Dr. B's office together. Caroline didn't feel trapped in her office anymore. She didn't feel like she wanted to run. She truly wanted to be there.

"I'm ready to talk," Caroline had said when she had first walked into the office.

So, they had talked. Caroline said everything. She didn't once hold anything back. Caroline talked about her mother asking her to stay. She still felt guilty about it, but it wasn't as bad as it had been before she had told anyone. Caroline talked about the Florida trip. Dr. B thought Bennett's choice for not staying together was honorable. Caroline had to agree. She finally understood. Caroline talked about being alone. She talked about every feeling that she felt when she was alone. *Breathe. Fix it. You're alone. You're going to die alone.* Caroline told Dr. B about trying the breathing exercises and that they helped sometimes.

"You know," Dr. B started, "whenever you have those feelings, everyone who loves you is only a phone call away."

And Dr. B was right. She was so right.

When their session was almost over, Caroline had to find the strength and bravery to do one last thing. "I need your help with something," Caroline said as Dr. B finished writing a note on Caroline's file.

"Oh?" Dr. B said, surprised.

Caroline opened up her bag and pulled out the bottle of pills. "Do you think you have time to sit with me?" Caroline's hands shook as she turned over her prescription.

Dr. B smiled. "We can do this another time if you're not ready, Caroline."

Caroline shook her head. "I have a panic disorder," Caroline started, finally naming her illness. Finally taking control. "It's time."

Dr. B nodded. Caroline opened her anxiety medicine and looked at the tiny pill in her hands. Her gramps had given her an epi-pen just in case. She had it in her bag. She told Dr. B about it. Dr. B let her know that it was good to be prepared, but also let her know the actual odds of her throat closing from those particular anxiety meds were slim to none. It made Caroline feel better even though her hands were still shaking just from holding the pill. Her throat felt so tight.

One. Two. Three. Four.

You can breathe.

You're not alone.

You're okay.

"You ready?" Dr. B asked.

Caroline looked at the yellow walls. For the first time, she didn't think about what color was beneath the yellow. She didn't see black. She only saw what was really there. She nodded at Dr. B as she took the pill and put it into her mouth, taking a sip of water to swallow it.

***

Mr. Johnson, her yearbook teacher, smiled down at her as she gathered up her senior class for pictures. Caroline was extremely proud of the theme for her senior yearbook. After everything that had happened, it just seemed right.

"Alright everyone!" she said in her leader voice. She felt nerves ripple through her, but took deep breaths to keep them at bay. "Let's form a line here so we can take the pictures."

Every single person in her senior class was dressed up in an outfit that reflected their career choice. She had explained to them before they set up this picture day that she wanted to reflect each person in their senior class as who they were based off of the choices they made. No one choice was correct for each person. Everyone had their own choice to make, and Caroline wanted to show that in the yearbook. It was similar to what she had done for Bennett's senior year, but this time, though, Caroline wanted the yearbook to not just use words to explain each graduate's choice. She wanted pictures.

Lined up for the pictures were mechanics, chefs, doctors, nurses, zookeepers, writers, architects, photographers, painters, teachers, welders, and so many other professions. It made Caroline smile to see each and every one of them as she took their picture. Some of them held up college acceptance letters. Some held up certificates for the programs they had trained for already.

When it was Caroline's turn, she held up her acceptance letter to FSU. She was dressed as a pharmacist. When she had left for school that morning, her grandparents had cried. Caroline cried with them.

After all the seniors had their pictures taken, Caroline had spent an obscene amount of time working on the yearbook. Not because it was due soon—she still had weeks—but because she was so pumped up from the idea that she didn't even want to wait.

The cover of the yearbook read:
It's your future. It's your choice.

***

Graduation had come and gone without too many problems. Caroline and Izzy had taken more pictures together than should ever be allowed. Izzy and Nick were still together. They had decided that they'd try long distance. Caroline knew that it would be a roller coaster for them. After all, Izzy always felt things in highs and lows, never anything in between. But Caroline didn't have a doubt in her mind that they'd make it together if that's what they wanted.

Even the summer had passed by in a flash. Izzy, Caroline, and Nick had spent almost every waking moment together. They had so many adventures and so many times that they got on each other's nerves, but Caroline couldn't imagine life without them. They hadn't even moved away yet and they were already developing rotating schedules to visit each other in the various parts of the country where they had decided to go to college.

Caroline still hadn't spoken to Bennett since the trip to Florida. Every now and then, she had texted Bennett telling him that she hoped he was doing well. He would text back the same.

Gramps had told her that Bennett visited him in the hospital when he had his heart attack. He even brought daisies. It had made Caroline's heart swell even though they weren't together. She knew he was there for her even if he couldn't show it all the time. She knew they'd make it back to each other when it was time. She just wished that it *was* time.

Caroline was sitting on the state line into Utah in her backyard. She still had trouble being alone, but this wasn't the worst that it would get. At least her grandparents were inside. She still had a tough couple months ahead of her when she moved to Florida next week, though, and she wasn't necessarily looking forward to it.

It was so weird. It was a strange mixture of being on the verge of a panic attack and being so happy that she could cry. And she had definitely had panic attacks. The meds helped, though, and she was thankful for that. Izzy and her grandparents helped, too. Izzy had witnessed Caroline's panic attacks for the first time a couple of weeks ago and Caroline was surprised at how amazing Izzy had been. It made Caroline realize just how crazy it was to keep the attacks a secret from Izzy in the first place.

"Mind if I sit here?"

Caroline's head jerked up at the sound of his voice. It was Bennett. He was there. Next to her. Wanting to sit by her.

"I-I mean, I—" Caroline stuttered. "Yes."

Bennett smiled as he pushed his glasses up the bridge of his nose. His coffee-colored skin reflected the sun in a beautiful way. Caroline wanted so badly to reach out and touch him. To hold his hand. Anything.

They both sat quietly next to each other as they stared out into the distance. All of Utah was ahead of them. A vast expanse of space and time and so many other things. Caroline wanted so very much to stay in Arizona. To stay where she felt safe and nothing ever changed. She couldn't do that to herself any longer, though, no matter how scared she was.

"How have you been?" Caroline asked, trying to keep the desperation out of her voice. She had to pull together a lot of courage just to say those four words.

"I've been good. Really good," Bennett said, smiling into the distance. He looked down at her. "I talked to my parents. Told them everything I was feeling. Everything that Josh was feeling before he left us. I told them that I wanted to stay here and write. They were a lot more understanding than I thought they'd be. I think I underestimated them." He paused for a moment, thinking about something. "I think I underestimated their grief, too."

Caroline smiled down at her feet. "I'm happy for you, Bennett. I really am."

"And you? How have you been?"

She looked at him and suddenly felt like crying. She was leaving in a week. She would be leaving the place she had called home for almost twelve years. Caroline tried to smile. "I'm getting better," she said, which was the truth.

One. Two. Three. Four.

"I hear you're moving next week," Bennett said quietly.

Caroline looked over to him. "Who told you?" she demanded.

Bennett shrugged and chuckled. "I have my sources."

She began fidgeting with her shoelaces. "I'm scared," she said.

He was quiet for a moment, and then began to speak. "She never realized that her light had always been greater than her darkness, but it was in her darkness that she found her light."

"Who said that quote?" Caroline asked.

Bennett blushed a deep scarlet. "Just something I've been working on." He looked down at his own shoes as Caroline smiled to herself.

"Do you think—?" she started. "I mean, can we—?"

He looked over at her and held her hand. She felt warmth flood through her as he touched her. She never wanted him to pull away. She never wanted him to leave.

"It's not time yet, Caro," he said.

Caroline looked sadly out at the horizon. She respected his decision, and she knew why he had to make it. Caroline was one thousand times better than she had been on that trip to Florida, but she still had so much farther to go. She thought of something suddenly and broke out into a huge smile.

"Okay, *well*," she drew out the syllables in each word. "Just because we can't be together doesn't mean that we can't be *together*."

Bennett laughed. "What does that even mean?" Then he blushed. "Do you mean like friends with—with benefits—?"

"Ew, Bennett, no," she said as she shoved him playfully a little. "I guess that one's on me. I definitely could've worded that better."

"You think?"

She shoved him again and they both laughed.

"I mean, Bennett, that we can still be *friends*," Caroline said, but then pointed at his face. "No benefits involved."

Bennett smiled back at her. "I think we can do that."

Caroline sighed in relief. "Whew, good because I'm gonna need all the help I can get when I move next week."

He shook his head and chuckled. "Somehow, I know that you'll be just fine."

Caroline became a little more serious then. She sighed again, but wistfully this time. She laid her head on his shoulder, both of them still sitting up and staring at the horizon. "I'm sorry, Bennett. I shouldn't have made you feel like Josh did. I shouldn't have hurt you like that. I'm so sorry."

"I know, Caro. I know," he said as he laid his head on hers, "and it's okay. We keep going, right? Together."

"Together," she whispered.

***

That next week had come and gone just as fast as graduation and summer had. Caroline remembered it like it was yesterday. Izzy, Bennett, and Caroline's grandparents had come with her to the airport to see her off. They walked her all the way to security, but then couldn't go any further. Caroline's nerves and anxiety had been in overdrive even with the medication. Her heart had been going a million miles an hour. She had said goodbye to her grandparents. She had said goodbye to Izzy. Both goodbyes were tearful and made Caroline's breathing extremely uneven. It was time for Bennett's goodbye then.

"I—" Caroline had started, tears still streaming down her face. "I don't know if I can do this."

Bennett had wiped the tears from her eyes. People had been passing them without a second glance. The airport had been just as crowded as ever, but Caroline had only wanted to see Bennett. She had wanted him to block out the world.

"You *can* do this, Caro. Just look at what you've done already." He had pulled her into a hug. Caroline hadn't wanted him to ever let go.

"Will it ever be time for us?" Caroline had asked him.

"Soon," he had smiled.

Caroline had nodded, and then had started to walk away to get in line at security. She hadn't been able to tell him goodbye. At least not in those words. It had hurt too much to even say what she had said.

"Caroline!" she had heard someone call.

She had turned around to see Bennett running towards her. He had stopped in front of her, way closer than he had been before.

Caroline remembered looking up at him. She remembered seeing that look in his eyes. "Kiss me," she had said. "Bennett, kiss m—"

He had wrapped his hand around her face and the back of neck as he had pulled her close to kiss her. She had loved kissing him. She loved how it brought back feelings that she only felt before her mother died. She had loved how kissing him blocked out every other feeling, every other emotion, and simply made her mind blank. She had wanted him to fix her, but she had known they both couldn't put their broken pieces together to make one whole person. It just wouldn't work like that. He had been right about that. His broken pieces wouldn't fill the holes from her missing ones. They both had to learn how to be okay alone before they could learn how to be okay together. But they had come so far together. Maybe, Caroline had thought, maybe they were close to being okay. Maybe they were okay enough to be okay together.

"Come visit me?" she had asked.

He had smiled at her. "Of course."

Bennett, Izzy, and her grandparents had left after that, and Caroline had to navigate the airport alone. She was fine until she had gotten on the plane, but because of a kind flight attendant, she was able to make it through.

That had been nearly a month ago now. Caroline could remember every detail of those first couple weeks and the panic attacks that came with them. With the help of her grandparents, Izzy, and Bennett, she had been able to make it, though. She had a new therapist in Florida who was almost as amazing as Dr. B (almost). Caroline still needed time to determine how awesome her new therapist was, though. The medicine helped, too, and she was so glad that she was finally able to take them.

Caroline looked down at her phone to the barrage of text messages that had become a daily routine ever since she moved away.

TUES – 7:07 AM

Izzy: I hope you have the best morning ever! Call me if you need anything.

TUES – 7:23 AM

Grams: Good morning, sweetie! I love and miss you!

TUES – 7:25 AM

Gramps: I know your grams beat me to it this morning, but I love you, kiddo! I'll text first tomorrow and win. Then she won't be able to gloat all day....

TUES – 7:49 AM

Bennett: T-minus three days until I get to see you.

Caroline smiled at the texts. Her grandparents had turned their texting into a competition to see who told Caroline that they loved her first. Whoever said it first didn't have to do any chores the whole entire day. Gramps normally lost and Caroline thought it was hilarious. It brought a smile to her face every single morning.

Bennett had scheduled a flight to Florida for the Labor Day holiday and he was going to stay the entire long weekend. They were officially together again.

She had come so far, but there was still a long way to go. Her panic still got the best of her sometimes. She let the darkness in more times than she was proud of. What she *was* proud of, though, was that she was always able to make it go away. Even if she had to deal with her panic disorder for the rest of her life, she knew that she'd be okay. She had so many people to help her, to guide her through it.

She had everything that she needed. Thinking about it made her smile and reach up to touch the locket around her neck.

After that moment in the hospital with her gramps, everything had changed for Caroline. Her whole entire mindset had shifted. It wasn't like she was cured. It wasn't like she had just read the list and gotten better. It was a choice that she made. It was a choice to get better and to try harder. It was a choice to keep going. It was a choice to look at all the little things in life and pick the good ones—the *happy* ones—and focus on them, never letting them go.

Remember

Caroline and Elizabeth's Happiness List of All the Little Things

1. Cold weather
2. Cookies
3. Florida State University
4. Hugs
5. Gramps and Grams
6. Each other
7. Izzy
8. Our house
9. Christmas music
10. Daddy
11. The strength of my daughter
12. **Mom.**

Acknowledgments

Acknowledgments are always so hard for me to write. So many people help me on a daily basis that I get nervous writing these acknowledgments and leaving someone important out. Just know that if you've ever spoken to me, you more than likely have touched my life and my writing in some way. The people who deserve the most thanks, though, are, of course, my family. From the support of my parents, siblings, in-laws, husband, friends, to even the unconditional love of my dogs. These people have taught me to grow, to love, and to always *always* be kind to others and to myself. I'd like to also thank my thesis professors from NSULA who tirelessly worked with me on making *All the Little Things* perfect. Without their support and encouragement, this novel would not be what it is today. Lastly, I want to thank you for taking your time to read this novel. It means so much to me and all of the characters are so dear to my heart. I hope you loved them as much as I do, and if you did, please consider leaving a review so that others can enjoy this story as well.